T0123229

Flying Dreams

Obu Udejiji

authorHOUSE

AuthorHouse™
1663 Liberty Drive
Bloomington, IN 47403
www.authorhouse.com
Phone: 833-262-8899

© 2022 Obu Udejiji. All rights reserved.

No part of this book may be reproduced, stored in a retrieval system, or transmitted by any means without the written permission of the author.

Published by AuthorHouse 10/11/2022

ISBN: 978-1-6655-7023-7 (sc)
ISBN: 978-1-6655-7022-0 (hc)
ISBN: 978-1-6655-7021-3 (e)

Library of Congress Control Number: 2022916529

Print information available on the last page.

Scripture quotations marked KJV are from the Holy Bible, King James Version (Authorized Version). First published in 1611. Quoted from the KJV Classic Reference Bible, Copyright © 1983 by The Zondervan Corporation.

Any people depicted in stock imagery provided by Getty Images are models, and such images are being used for illustrative purposes only. Certain stock imagery © Getty Images.

This book is printed on acid-free paper.

Because of the dynamic nature of the Internet, any web addresses or links contained in this book may have changed since publication and may no longer be valid. The views expressed in this work are solely those of the author and do not necessarily reflect the views of the publisher, and the publisher hereby disclaims any responsibility for them.

Contents

This book is dedicated to Obu Christian Pancham and Obu Alexander Pancham.

Introduction

This book's purpose is to explain my flying dreams and share my knowledge and thoughts with the world and the intersection between the dream world and the real world, deciphering all the information flowing through me. Unfortunately, this will not be easy because most of the data from the dream world are encrypted; as we all know, everyone has a different dream world, and flying the dreams is mine. And the imagination, if I could bring all the beautiful things I see in the dream world to the real world and replace everyone's nightmare with flying dreams, my job is done here on earth. My purpose is to give human beings access to fly across the stars. The whole point of all this is to help humanity ultimately conquer the universe, to help Africa, Biafra, Nigeria, and the world.

Sometimes dream world can be overwhelming especially waking up to the world we know as the real world, but don't worry, sometimes I do not understand it myself, and life must go on. Unfortunately, I often fly in space, visiting different planets and stars. I have been to many plants and have experienced people sharing their life stories in other languages. This is reality; It is all in dreams.

There are some things in the dream world I will not allow to flow through; it's not the time for the world to recognize its existence; it is the will of life as everyone is different. And yet, here we are, living in the same world, trying to understand each other. Some governments struggle to put food on the table for their people and hold their country together even in chaos. In contrast, other organizations claim to be responsible for the world's ups and downs and prosperity. The earth is overpopulated, they say; I never quite understood that; on top of that, we are still trying to find who we are, or if there is anyone or anything out there, searching for the truth to understand life. But the fact is given turn by turn.

I do not believe in coincidence. I have lived for a long time, enough to know that everything happens for a reason. One reason could be your destiny, and the other might be an error. Everything was created in balance. The truth was right in front of us all this while. Sometimes, our mistakes lead us to see what is coming and what the universe installed for us. The universe is always watching us. Constantly. It is the center of the origin of humankind. Everyone contributes to it. Even in Genesis, God says to let us create man in our image and spirit. That means he didn't make everything alone. He had some help; there are others, as Jesus Christ during the creation, but the Father is the alpha. As I said, you cannot have one without the other. One is always more significant than the other. Here you have God and Satan, Man and Woman, water and fire, Heaven and earth, moon and sun; one is always more significant, yet you can't have one without another.

The planet was created to coexist, multiply in numbers, and have dominion over all things. We did our best to live and sustain our lives. We are all part of survivors. When life in the real-world tires and vexes me, I will sleep. Hopefully, I can spend one week in my dream world for one night and find some peace. There is nothing more beautiful in the universe than flying in dreams.

This book contains three things: flying dreams, building Nigeria, and building machines to help humanity. These three are things of the future to come. The brightest future for everyone. For every living being on earth.

The idea for this book is to make the world a better place, nothing more, nothing less. I want every child, every woman, and man to have equal rights; it's the only way to find out who we are and where we come from. We will be greater than we are now. Reaching out to the stars means touching each other in need, love, and happiness. There is no other way. The idea of one person having more money than a whole country will be eliminated, releasing that country's civilization from slavery and freeing them from global political-economic imprisonment. There will be no more than one person swimming in billions of dollars while half the world suffers.

Do you think God will allow us to know where we come from and who we are if we haven't acknowledged the pain the world is suffering? Or the pain each of us suffers inside? Or if we do not realize the truth about humanity and every living thing on earth? No, he will not allow it. Until we have loved each other, we will never find the truth of who we are and how we got here without speculations. We were going in the right direction, but now we are just fading into oblivion, living like tomorrow doesn't exist. And most of us no longer know our purposes.

The strong prey on the weak and forget the repercussions and consequences of evil are right behind them. They will come to collect. The same way you measure for others is how it will be calculated for you. Until we realize we are going in the opposite direction, turn back, and go the other way.

I am not against science. They can research, find out what they can to help us stay alive and where we come from, and keep watch over the sun for solar flames, aliens, or whoever is coming to kill us outside God's commandments. I am not against them. It is cheaper to make Planet Earth a paradise than to travel to Mars to build a new city. The latter will cost the world dearly and increase inequality. It will destabilize the mechanical roots of the world's economy, crippling it and creating a more significant gap between the rich and the poor. And if the rich travel to another planet, Planet Earth is nothing more than a garbage bin for those left behind. On Mars, they can start anew with all the money they took. Those left behind can die here on earth, or they can make us FFs—famous farmers—for them. The beautiful part of a rich man living on Mars is that he will probably live forever; at least, that is what he hopes. But the time difference between Mars and Earth is not much; everyone dies. What matters the most is how you live your life among your neighbors.

I am not saying that expeditions and colonization of Mars are terrible ideas. I am just saying, "We have to sweep inside the house first before we sweep outside"; my mother used to say that. It means you must take care of your home first before taking care of outsiders. Or you can take care of your family first before you take care of outsiders. That is what I am saying. Think about it. Imagine if all the rich people on earth take everything, live on Mars, and interrupt the ecosystem. The setback will be catastrophic.

Chapter 1

Flying in The Dream World

I will start from the beginning before I fly into space. I was just here on earth. When I flew for the first time in my dreams, I ran. Hundreds of people were trying to kill me. I didn't know what was happening, but my entire body was flying. I was so high in the sky that no one could catch me. I flew to a cassava farm. It was a new plane for me to enter, another realm. In this realm, you can do anything: walk, swim, even fall in love or find endless happiness.

Then I came upon a farm and saw a partridge caught in a trap and struggling. I didn't know if I had released it; I just remembered it was there. I spent a couple of days on that farm in a dream. I grew tired; I couldn't lift into the sky. Luckily, I was on a hill, which allowed me to descend and stretch out my wings. And I started flying farther and farther away until I woke up.

The next night I flew across the ocean. I flew over the tree lines. I landed in a beautiful place with grass, trees, and fruit. Both rotten fruit and good fruit; some fell to the ground, some still attached to the trees ripped like mangos, there a maze farm stretched almost a mile, I spent a couple of weeks there, or even years in the dream world, trying to fly away. I did everything I could, but it was no use. I decided to wait, thinking that *maybe this was where I was meant to be.* But it didn't feel like I was supposed to be there. So, I continued to wait for the time to come when I could move on. I don't think I had a destination in mind; I knew I was going to a place but not *here*. I began to think maybe I had just stopped there to rest.

Then suddenly, I saw a ship waiting to take me farther north. After the boat docked, everybody—including me—disembarked. I didn't know where I was.

One afternoon I was resting and fell asleep. I remember that I started to fly again, deeper into space. I did not see myself on land as I usually do. Nor did I know where I was going to land. Then I appeared in a silver stone temple, with water flowing upstream from the stone. There was a bench made of stone; it was like a living room space and shrine. I did not know if it was a shrine, but I knew the place was a temple. I heard the people talking.

The first thing I heard was about a visit from a god. One of the gods visited the temple, but I do not know whether it was God. Some people were sitting on the bench; a child sat beside them. I did not know exactly who the child was, but it was a boy. Then I heard some of the masters coming toward me, arguing. One of them asked, "How did this happen?"

One said, "She must come back; we must bring her back." They started to talk about what was going on. There was a pregnant woman about to give birth to a son. Some men had deceived her, and they took her away. She trusted them and had no fear that they would harm her. But their true intentions were to eat the baby and kill the woman. The baby possessed the highest power. How do I know that? Because one of the masters said so.

While I was there, I saw a vision. I was not sleeping. Everything would be destroyed if the child did not return to the temple.

I saw the sun breaking apart in that vision and breaking apart like it would crack open. I looked up again and saw two planets facing each other. They were like the earth, but the world is full of vegetation, and the ocean color makes it blue and green. These two planets facing each other were the color of ice planets (which I will explain later), yet it was not cold. They shook as if there were earthquakes. But the master said the universe's balance had been altered, so they were stunning.

Still, I saw the monsters trying to eat the baby when it was born in the vision. Afterward, I told the masters my dream, and they sent two men on a brown horse, each wearing a red cape, traveling at high speed to pursue the mother and boy. After I explained my vision, I was scared and thirsty. My whole body was shaking, and I had goosebumps. Then I went upstream to the stone from which the water was coming. I tried to drink the water, but I was so scared. Part of me said, Drink the water because I am thirsty, and part said, do not drink it because something bad might happen. So, I looked back to the bench where I had been sitting to see whether the older man was still sitting with the child. The older man was gone, but the child was still there. I said, "No, I will not drink the water I say to myself.

I flew out into space. I could see the planets together, facing each other and cracking in the center with the stone falling on the bottom. You could see the energy flowing from the bottom to the planets. I flew away and woke up on earth.

I woke up in the real world, drank water, cleaned my apartment, and napped again. I started to fly again in the dream world. This time I was on the earth's surface. But then suddenly I was flying in the sky. I decided to go to Africa to see my mother.

When I reached Africa, I saw my mom sitting with a friend in front of the house. Somehow, I was able to talk to her. She could hear me and recognize my voice. I could see her. The expression on her face seemed to ask, *why are you like this? Why do you look like this?* It could have meant something else, but that is what I thought she was thinking. Then the voice came to me: "I ask tell me why I can hear your mother. A new system has been created that will affect every man, woman, and child on earth; the same system impacts the dream world. That's why you can hear your mother, allowing

3

the traveler who flies in the dream to speak and talk to individuals. But the system is dangerous." The voice kept saying, echoing as I flew further away.

Then I saw some of my village men standing on the street. I asked how they were doing, and they also recognized my voice. They called my name. Then suddenly, I saw them passing out as if they were dying. The voice had said earlier that the system was dangerous, and it was right. I tried asking the voice what his name was; who are you? He never answered me, so I gave him a reputation as an agent. According to the agent, the system would destroy the world. I asked, "Why is the system affecting them? Why am I talking to people in the dream whom I usually don't talk to? And in the dream, they can recognize me?" And the agent said the system was created as an implant attached to the DNA of every person.

At this point, an old woman told me I had no idea who she was: "If you start to fly away from this place, they will get better because the system has not corrupted them yet." So, I flew away, and when I looked back, they were getting better.

To understand both dreams, you must remember that they were just dreams. You can understand as much as possible and interpret as much as you want. But information can never be accurate if you have received or given information about what is to come, especially what people talk about in the movies. Dreams are more like a code, a hint, an insight of what is to come. To know is to accept and embrace it, no matter the fear.

Based on my understanding and beliefs, I must first apologize if what I am about to say offends or makes you uncomfortable. I am sorry about that. I have watched men and women who claim to understand everything about life judge me based on their knowledge about me. I have watched them conspire to taint my name. But I can guarantee that I already know how it ends for them. Silence is the best answer for a fool. You can say I am rude; I am an asshole. I don't care. Those are human phrases for people who disagree with your knowledge and ideologies.

Do you remember me telling you that the truth is given turn by turn? When the time comes, you will know the truth about everything, including the flying dream, the real world, the migrations, the animals, and every living thing. I cannot tell you what my truth is. I have an answer, but it's for me and me alone. Even though the fact does not seem to matter now, give it time. You will see it because it is about enjoying yourself in this physical life and forgetting to feed your soul or spirit; you throw all your eggs in one basket. The food for your soul is the kindness you show towards another human being, the love you share with all creation. In this era, everyone wants to be something. I am here and have seen it for years. I have seen human hearts and understand the greediness of humankind and its selfishness. Which always leads to conflict, desolation, and poverty. In my understanding, the truth is that I am a human just like you but with an extraordinary gift.

Have you ever heard of soldier ants? Well, they are a vicious kind. When they are threatened, they fight to the death to defend the colony they belong to. Soldier ants are one of the most organized species and have developed a communication type we humans can not comprehend.

As a traveler of more than sixteen countries and thirty cities, I can tell you I have watched humans do horrible things to each other in the name of survival or power. I always try to understand every country I go to and their ways of life, no matter how long I spend there. Some places see me as their savior. I can see it in their eyes. They are looking for a savior to save them from whatever is troubling them. My answer is always the same: I cannot be a savior. It is too much for one man with no resources. I have two thousand people in the village who are counting on me. I cannot stay in another country and be a savior. I don't have the capacity or the power to do that. I can only pray for them and release them from their guilt of sin, which they thought was the cause of their suffering.

I don't know if you believe in heaven and hell. If I look into my heart, I will see the beauty of creation. And when I look around, I see all the magic and miracles. It is not like the heaven you have imagined. So, children of God, you can change your situation. You can fly with hidden wings from human eyes and go anywhere you want without boundaries.

I wish I could show you the city of stars. I have been there. You cannot go to Saturn in real life. Saturn is the master of all control and the firstborn during the creation of the universe. If you fly too close, it will pull you to itself. If I am supposed to live a thousand years, I will live on Saturn. It is one of my favorite planets. From there you can fly to the glass planet, the most beautiful planet I have ever seen. I was there for many months.

I never got to spend as much time as I wanted to on Saturn, just a few minutes. What I was looking for was not there. There is nothing there for me except a resting place. I am always in search of a blue crystal stone on Saturn. I searched all of Saturn, and there was no stone. I just wanted to see it amid the sparkling space and imagine how beautiful it would be shining across the stars.

It took forty-five seconds to get from Saturn to Mars on some nights. There are people there—lots of them. I believe in some parts of science but do not believe what they say about Mars. You can believe me or not, but I am telling you the truth. My ancestors are there. If you are looking for material worth on this planet, you will not find much. It is not there if you are looking for a place to acquire knowledge. You are looking in the wrong place. Instead, look into your heart. You will find what you are looking for if your heart is genuine.

I do not remember if I talked about this earlier in the book, but the truth must be answered. I must tell you the truth. Even though I said I would wait, I will tell you *my* truth. We are in a new age. I have seen the war. You might doubt me, but it is a fact, and the battle is here. Three years ago, while flying in the dream world, I saw a black ship at the space station, collecting materials and parts that made up the space station and converting them to red, melted soil that rained entirely over the whole earth, like hot mud. People were screaming and crying in pain.

When I convert what I saw to what is happening today in the real world, I see coronavirus, COVID-19. We cannot see it, but it is there. This is just the beginning. The world will never be the same after this. Trust me. In the dream world, the war ended. Humans did not win the war. The same thing is happening in the real world with COVID-19. Humans cannot win against this virus.

During the war in the dream world, I was flying in the sky when I saw a giant snake. Lightning came from his mouth. He slithered on the ground, ripping it up, swallowing people, and destroying everything in its path. I dived back, grabbed as many people as possible, and flew away. I tried taking as many people as possible who could keep up with me. The human race survived in the end, but there was nothing left.

I found myself in the mountains with an older woman I had never met. She said the war had ended, but another one was coming—a new war. Five years before the recent war, I saw the heavens split into two parts. Half of the sky was a blue sky, and the other half was a white sky. There was writing on both halves. One was written in black ink and English. It read, "standard timest." The other half was written in red ink and Arabic. Within fifteen seconds, I saw the one written in Arabic ripple together and explode all over the earth. One piece fell on my leg, and I cleaned it off.

It is not that simple when you try to translate all of this into the real world. You must first understand that you cannot control what others do or say but can control what you do or say. The same applies to flying dreams. The planet is ours. We have sacrificed so much in this world, war after war, killing each other for land and minerals in the real world, to build our world the way it is today. We have regulations and bylaws to keep everyone safe. And we have discovered and invented machines that cause more harm than good in finding out who we are. This includes technologies that help us but have created dangerous wastes, like radiation, that will also kill us. I am surprised we have managed to control wastes, including those produced by radioactive power plants.

There is one thing that gives me sleepless nights: the internet. This is just my opinion; The internet controls 70 percent of our lives. We depend on it for everything, and that is a scary thing. Can you imagine if something happened to the internet? Our world would fall back into the dark ages. All our systems are run by software and hardware—the computer and the internet control even money printing. We should find another way just in case of unexpected events.

As an African scholar, I know this knowledge was established as fact. To be clear, before I proceed, this has nothing to do with God. This is my experience from the dream world to real life and the differences between both worlds. Dreamworld visions are happening, have happened, or will happen. As a human, you learn from your experiences and mistakes. That is how you know where to look when facing something you have encountered. Things from the past are lined up like a checkbox.

It is hard to speak about something you cannot prove. In Africa, Nigeria, and the east, in my birth home in the mountains, flying in your dreams is considered witchcraft, especially if you have access to both worlds. They call you a witch because they are the only people who can fly in the sky. But having the gift of flying in your dreams is a gift, a gift from God alone as far as I am concerned. It is not an astral projection, as some people call it.

The only way we can navigate the axis key is to know the location of the center point. There is always a center point. Nothing is impossible to achieve in this world. God has given us all the tools and knowledge to design and create a better world. That's why he made us the superintendents of earth. But he expects more from us, and we must do better. Our prayers might not be answered if we pray to God for wealth alone. So pray for wisdom and knowledge; that is wealth. I do not pray like everyone else. My prayers are from the heart. They are full of energy, which means I can choose to kneel or not. I can see the power of God through prayer. There is a relationship between God and me.

In John 16:20 -30[1] from the Holy Bible, King James Version, God says, "whenever a woman is in labor, she has pain, because her hour has come; but when she gives birth to the child, she no longer remembers the anguish because of the joy that a child has been born into the world." God says she is the same with you now, you in grieve, this grief will be turned into joy, just as what happens with the woman in labor. And he promises that somewhere in psalms 91 God says "he will give the angels charge concerning you, to guard you in all your ways. They will bear you up so you do not strike your foot against the stone."[2] Still, John 16 all way 30, somewhere there, he says, I will give you whatever you want, everything you ask of me, you will be full of joy, and you will have nothing more to ask because I have given you all of your heart's desires. In my translation and understanding, all these means is that you must do your part, hustle hard, and you shall have it. Always believe because you are from the light. Even though there is darkness, a single light shines from a distance, destroying the darkness. So you see, brothers and sisters, do not be afraid. We are the winners.

The accuracy of narrating the dream world's meaning to the real world is based on the dreamer. In my experience, my accuracy is categorized based on what is happening in my life in the real world and how the pattern works in the dream world. Most of the time, the

---

[1] Psalm 91:11–12.
[2] Psalm 91:11–12.

result is accurate. The dream world is usually on a different plane. I do not know if I mentioned this previously, but I will repeat it. There is a hidden world, a beautiful world. It is a place where you can rest. There are no rules or laws, not even uncertainty. There are no predicaments. This world is a free place. I am not saying it is a total paradise, but it is beautiful enough to make your soul rejoice. There is something I call "unexpected obstructions" in life that make a mess and change things. They make you feel like you are not in control, even though you know you are in control. It would help if you never forgot you created these obstructions, whatever you feel; you alone allowed them to exist. You can eliminate them whenever you want.

I hold on to having all the lines of my flying dreams, understanding and researching what I have learned so far in the dream world and real worlds. But I need to find the perfect time to explain everything to you. I do not want to add any of that to this book. It is bigger than me, more prominent than everything you have ever been led to believe. I need to explain what it means, but not in this book. I will tell you everything in the next book. I will find the strength to say to you all about it at the end. You need to know all that has happened in the dream world. I have met close friends, some lovers, some beautiful ones passing by, and those who have come to calm me. Those who call you tell you to take a rest. I have told them about their dreams. They are not allowed to speak about it to anyone. The consequences are greater than they can imagine. It will not affect me if they tell someone; it will affect them. The problem is that I cannot watch them suffer from something they do not understand, so I am obliged to find a solution because it will also affect me. So, they mustn't tell anyone until the time is right.

The influence of the dream world can hijack your mind if you fight it, but only if you are a dreamer and you know they are separate things. Some people do not dream at all. So, if you are a dreamer— like the young ones trying to understand their dreams—it is not the same as the others who have mastered their dreams but are sometimes wrong in their translations, and their narratives are not always the same. The only person who can explain goals is the dreamer. Two things can be done if the dreamer does not understand their dreams. The dreamer can either expel the dream or create a new consciousness for the invention, a different way to understand it based on their mindset, which automatically reverses the original copy of the dream from the dreamer's mind, especially if it's a bad dream.

For the young dreamers, be careful how you choose to remember your dreams when you awake. It can damage your mindset if you do not understand your vision. Be sure to write it down as soon as you open your eyes. If not, it can lead you in another direction. Do not be afraid. Ultimately, you always end up where you are going, not where you are coming from.

This usually happens to young dreamers who do not know how it works. It is like science. For example, when there is lightning or a thunderstorm. Or when you walk on the street, it seems you have been there before, like déjà vu. I call these memories of another plane-like stimulation. That is why younger dreamers do not understand it. I have been there. I know how frustrating it can be. I know because I can see it. Knowledge is power. Greater than money.

When I was going to school, I was not doing so to get a degree or a job. I wanted to learn how people saw themselves. Knowledge is power, and I have it. Every human being on earth has expectations about knowledge. As a dreamer, you must listen to what they are saying. Collect all the information you can accumulate.

There are three types of countries. Stage 3 is for those who must depend on world aid for survival. Those in stage 2 find solutions to their problems by inventing things, including oilfield equipment, mining equipment, transportation, and social systems, to help them grow. And finally, stage 1 countries have almost 70 percent of the world's resources.

Chapter 2

Flying with The Universe

We must ensure that everything is balanced in the real world because existence is not the same as in the dream world. Reality is complex in the real world, especially if you do not know where you belong. The dream and real worlds coexist on different planes but in the same place. So, there are more challenges than you could ever imagine. My advice? None of this is your fault. Most of the time, the cause of our suffering is the collision of both worlds.

Do the best you can, and leave the rest for the universes. If you genuinely want something hard to achieve, the universe will help you achieve it. Use your judgment based on the information you have. Despite all the inconveniences and setbacks, we purposely sabotage ourselves to belong, be accepted, and be loved. And yet no one can see your heart or what your soul desires and craves. How do I know this? Because I have been through it. My purpose is to help humankind. I want to give something out of all I have known and seen. There are things I know that I cannot speak about. This is what I can give to humankind. Hopefully, one day someone will figure out the easy way to achieve it.

Life is not black and white or as it appears to be. Some people on this earth will stop at nothing but ruin your happiness. Trust me; there's evil in this world. I should not use the word "evil." It is a strong word. Instead, I will call them mean people. They are like vultures and thieves waiting for you to win. And once they see you have won, they will try to snatch it away from you.

All I want to do is to help humanity. I have seen the struggle and suffering of my family and my village in Africa. As a child, I used to imagine myself as one of the wealthiest men on earth to help everyone, that just a child's imagination, anything is possible, and now I settle for hope and making miracles.

My father always told us stories of men who traveled across Nigeria, hunting for animals and bringing them home for the villagers. A metaphor came along with the stories: If you haven't shared your wealth with the people in the village, your wealth belongs to one, and no one knows your name or that of your father. As I grew up, I realized we no longer hunt for animals; we hunt for money. That is my desire to help the poor, especially in Africa. No one knows how hard it is for some villages that have been forgotten and lost in time. My only wish is to bring them into the modern world. They will be forgotten forever if they do not come into the contemporary world. So you see, I have more to worry about than increasing gas prices or disappointment when my wife does not say hello or ask how my day went.

War, death, and poverty destabilize the modern world; that is the truth. My second home is in Canada. It is a rich country that does not need anything from me. My desire to help also comes with a price of fair judgments based on who needs my help the most. And not because you are my relative or a family member; that makes you think you are entitled to my assistance before anyone else. My judgments and decisions are based on the information I have from the people in the village and friends and families I can trust. With that information, I make decisions without regret. I do not care if you categorize me as a savage or a hero. I do not care if you do not like me, hate me, or even love me. It matters not to me because I have something you do not: I have the ultimate gift, which allows me to find out who needs my help the most. And that person shall be helped first. There is a benefit in helping the poor because it is the fruit of my soul.

I see everyone taking care of their bodies. For example, they eat good food and go to the gym. But they forget to feed their souls. Over time the soul will starve and ultimately become something else. So, there is no way you can ignore the state of your being from its origin to later in life.

Family is not just important. It is everything. Some of us belong with our families, and some choose not to have a family. In my experience, a person cannot be whole without their family. The problem is that families often do not appreciate each other. That is where doubt begins to ripple into the spouse's mind and the questions of who has your back at the end. When life gets tough, the only person you need at that moment is your partner. My father always used to say, "Imagine that your life is a bumpy road; if you have a smooth road, that is a bonus." If you see your life as bumpy, then there is nothing you cannot achieve or become in life because you already know failure is just of many lessons. And you will not be afraid of attempting the impossible. In the end, we are all winners.

Some people still keep their high school friends until they are older. It is part of belonging. The human mind and body were not designed to be alone, wandering like sheep without their shepherd. That is not how humans were made. Some find true love and hold on to it without letting go, even though love is the most expensive and dangerous in the universe. Do not get me wrong; love is beautiful. A husband and wife belong with their children, as the creator intended us to be. Separating them will have devastating consequences and leave wounds that might not heal for a lifetime. The children pay the ultimate price.

Here in Canada, where I live, family law is one of the most complex family laws I have ever seen. In my journey as an African scholar, if I were ever asked for my opinion of it, I would suggest they amend family law to help hold families together so that the children can enjoy a lifetime of parental love. In my opinion, what happens here in Canada, most people are depressed, and there is a high rate of mental disorders among Canadians aged twenty-nine to forty-five, including single moms and dads. It is sad to watch family members looking for a new family while they already have one. But the law forces them to do so due to mistakes made by the parents. No one is perfect; no one has it all figured out. Everyone has their issues, and there is a mess of emotions. This is normal, but it is not enough to separate the families. I am not saying people should be stuck in abusive relationships. I am saying the law is doing more damage than providing help. Children are not the only ones who need discipline. Sometimes adults need discipline as well, but without interference of any kind from outsiders unless bodily harm is caused. It is sad for a man to know that all his troubles come from those he loved and cared for. In Canada, having a child is like committing a criminal offense, with no disrespect to mothers and fathers. I am one too,

It is worst for those who come to Canada in adulthood because they have to adjust to the law and the culture. One mistake, and they are doomed. I always thought that if I could write what I felt and all that was in my mind, it would help me break free from this world. But it does not work like that. Did you know there is pain that wouldn't go away? From the time it will bring bad days. And there is the sadness I call these legendary bad days. These are the worst of the bad days. It is tough to remember the bad days when good days are in play; that does not mean those bad days were not there; they still are. Sometimes I do not understand this world based on where we are or where we are coming from, with the different cultures, names, and personalities. And wherever you go, you must start all over again.

My father used to say, "When a man dies, he turns to dust." No one thinks of his social class, material wealth, or popularity. When you die, it is the end. It does not matter if you loved someone or someone loved you. The only thing that matters is that you are dead and are in a grave. If you are lucky, you will get flowers from loved ones. Flowers are plants, and they die, usually in twenty-four hours. That is all you get. Some people do not even get flowers. They are forgotten. As time goes by, everyone will ignore them.

What I am trying to say is that life is precious. Everyone should be cautious not to throw away their freedom or let the enemy steal it. There should be good and evil in normal circumstances, but it does not work like that in real life. Not even in the dream world. Sometimes humans are the evil ones. Have you seen God? Of course not. No one has seen God. Have you seen the devil? No one has seen the devil either; you need to pay attention here; God and Satan use the same method to save or destroy someone. When God wants to help you, he sends someone; when Satan wants to harm you, he sends someone, so you up to you to figure out all people in your life what they stand for and cut off those that come to harm you.

Another thing is your perception of life in general; This has nothing to do with God or Satan. It is just you and how you perceive things and your anger and frustration that drag you to do the things you do. Everyone knows what is wrong and what is right.

I am in pain today. I can say it is one of the worst days. I am not blaming anyone for it. It is just another thing I have experienced in this life. You can run all you want, but trust me, whatever happens to you, your likes, and disappointments always come from those close to you. A person can be walking on the street, doing their own thing, and someone who doesn't know you will hate you or want to try to kill you for no reason. Sometimes it is someone from your own family or others you cared for. They are the ones trying to destroy you, and you allow them. They do not know the meaning of love. Nor do they understand it. All they want to do is to get even for whatever they perceive you have done to them. It does not matter if you are right or wrong.

In this part of the world, your opinion or your side of the story does not matter. You will be blamed even if you are right. Maybe it is because of your skin color or your mind's attributes. I cannot quite understand it. Most of the time, I wonder, how can you hate a person who has done nothing wrong to you? Just hate them. Is it because of the way they look? To me, it is disgusting. But life goes on. What can I say? Sometimes things are taken too far. And some look like vultures, trying to pick your flesh while you are still alive. And thieves behind your back trying to get what they can. It makes me wonder, what is life? No one understands that if you take food away from someone in the East, someone in the West will lose their chance of stopping hunger and vice versa.

There is a world between this world and the dream world. Some group or organization thinks it knows everything about some part of Planet Earth. They try to control everyone and tell them what to do. They implement laws that are so difficult to follow. It brings more pain. And if you are not careful about enforcing the law, the problem will destroy all you have built. It takes one angry man only a second to destroy everything he has made over the years. Generally, people do not get mad unless something has happened to them. And if something happens to them, there may not be anything that can make it okay—except getting even.

So, brothers and sisters, I urge you to be very careful how you treat others, as everyone has demons in them. We need to work hard so that none of us release the demons from their cages. They only come out when you are oppressed or destroyed, or someone tries to take something precious to you. This can drive you to cross the line. Grit does not matter when you are in pain. People often think that revenge is not the same as vengeance, but revenge is pretty much the same as vengeance. And to top it off, revenge is the same as justice. But does having justice make it ok? No, it does not. It takes people like me to understand that revenge and justice matter none if you have something very precious. Protect it at all times because when you lose it, it is gone, and no amount of justice can make it ok.

I cannot fly in the real world as I fly in the dream world. But I know one thing for sure: I can destroy someone who hurt me without touching them. But who am I to carry out such judgments? If you ruin someone, you must first judge that individual in your heart. It does not matter if you are right or wrong. The only things in your mind are the pain and the desire to get even. Well, do not get even; it will not make things OK. Some people have hurt me in this world, stolen from me, lied to me. We have all suffered greatly. What can I say? I can destroy them, even without touching or going near them. That I allowed them to live is my divine power. Like when a spider is in the room and a girl is sleeping. Some girls are scared of spiders and ask a man to kill them. Some men kill the spider, and others trap them in a cup and release them to live elsewhere. I am saying there are so many ways to solve an issue without hurting one in the process, and God will show you the same kindness that you have offered to those who hurt you and continue to do so. When you are angry, your mind is blind. You might be judging people for something that you did. It is not wise to judge anyone on something you might be guilty of. I am tired. Exhausted. I do not understand why I am being hurt by those I love and care for.

No one can tell us what life is hiding or what is ahead. You cannot see me tomorrow. No one can see it tomorrow. Tomorrow is better than today. There is no way to beat up a child and ask him not to cry. That is just wrong. It does not work that way.

Today I am speaking my mind. I am not building the country of Nigeria, trying to help the poor, or trying to reason with the rich. No, not today. Today I am in pain. Not physical pain, emotional pain. Punishments of the heart are sometimes worse than punishments of the body. When someone cuts you with a blade, you can feel pain. But it lasts longer than you know when someone hurts you from the inside. When someone cuts your skin, you can heal. But your heart will take time, and the pain stays there. No one can understand your feelings because they are not in your shoes.

When I was a child, I wanted to help others. When I saw the poor suffering, it hurt me. And when I saw the pain of this world or when young ones were misled, I felt their pain, including those lovely ones who did not understand how much evil in the world. The only way to help is through kindness and inspiration.

I believe in God, though I sometimes doubt God exists. Should I fight for everything I have lost, or should I get even with everyone who has wronged me? Sometimes I do not think there is judgment for anyone. Who is judging whom?

I do not want to believe the scientists. They believe that life originated from the big bang. Let's look at it this way. If they are correct, there is only one kind of life. If a tree manifested from the big bang, it would be a tree. It will just be humans if a human, not a thousand diverse living things on land and in the sea and air. That makes no sense to me. Besides, life means much more than a burning rock that fell from the sky.

All creation is from God, yet God is not here to help us in our times of trouble. What can I say? It falls on me to remind everyone that we are precious in creation. When bad things happen to you, how you respond is the only thing that matters. Let it sink in first until you can see clearly what happened. Especially in a situation where you are innocent, don't fall into the trap of payback, or you will doom yourself to unhappiness and become the one who suffers the consequences because of your actions. I try not to respond the way people expect me to respond.

So, you see why I called today a legendary lousy day. Bad days, worse days, sad days, and depressed days. Today is one of the most miserable days for me. We live and love, enjoying life for whatever it is worth. I do not know if there is a God or not; the only way I will know if God exists is after I am dead. Until then, I will do whatever pleases me. And when I die, I will find out if there is judgment for the evil people do to each other. I do not understand how people can be heartless. All they want to do is take and take until there is nothing more to take. They then throw everyone in the trash like they were nothing. You are better than you think or what society projects you. They just want you to feel that way, so you do not know who you are. My advice is not to let evil people change who you are. I don't live by the same rules as society expects me to. Remember who you are. You were born with pure love and created by the right hand of God. You are of the light, not of the darkness. Even the Bible says it is OK for me to get mad when people wrong me. But I am also told you should not carry that anger with me. You must always forgive before the sun sets. Then you can go to bed and sleep peacefully.

There are things in this life you can say and never take back. And your words can hurt innocent people. Remember that anger is the opposite of happiness. No matter how angry you are, you can be happy as well. Another opposite of happiness is regret. So, it is difficult to be fully happy if you hurt the innocent. Each time you are delighted, regret can snatch it away from you. So be careful, brothers and sisters. Do not be too quick to anger and take revenge against those who wronged you. I beg you to listen to your mind. Sometimes the truth is not far from the lies. You cannot have one without the other. Trust me when I say, "It is better to forgive than to get even." Sometimes you might be wrong and not understand that getting even is the same as the crime itself. So be careful and be compassionate toward each other. Do not allow yourself to break your beliefs' restrictions and boundaries.

Most of us already know what we will do or be when we grow up or what part of this world will be our domain, mainly if our parents have already paved the way for them. Even if some have a passion for something else, it may be a family tradition to carry on. It might be a grandfather's business to pass on to the next generation. It is already there for you; it is not like running away from your destiny. People always say that it is a choice, and it has always been a choice. Even though some don't believe it, it is what it is.

Destiny is more dangerous than choice. If you don't know it, it might take the wrong direction, and then you find yourself in a place where you ask yourself, "How did I get here?" But the choice is not the same. You can choose whichever way you want to go. Sometimes with that choice, things do not turn out exactly how you expected, but at least you were in charge. In the end, it all means the same thing. The difference with destiny is that it will come with a choice, but you must work hard for it. In the end, fate and choice sometimes arrive at the same place.

Every human has a purpose in life. Your life has no meaning if you think you do not have a purpose. You can choose whatever purpose you want or need. In this life, the objective is everything. Yes, it would help if you had something to give. That is how I see it. Most people would call it stupid just to give everything away. But they often misunderstand me.

In my case, I am not here to help you achieve your dreams or make you a rich man or woman. You have to do that yourself. I am here to support you in any way I possibly can.

That I can, do not expect me to give you or teach you how to be a millionaire overnight. That is not why I am here. I am here to guide using the knowledge and resources that I have. And when you are restless at night, there is a place you can go in the flying dream world to cool off from this reality. From there, you can figure out how to achieve your dreams. Not just to be rich in money but also in knowledge and happiness.

I have been there myself, and I have them both to give. In my knowledge and over time, I have learned so much through my travels and as an African scholar. Among them, whatever you want, you can have. To become something greater other than yourself requires hard work and commitment. Anything good does not come for free. Nothing is free. Everything worth something has a price.

Nothing can make me happy. No one in this world can make me happy. I am happiness itself. I have completed my peace, and it is OK. I have learned that those who hate you will sacrifice their happiness to make you unhappy and forget that joy comes from the inside. It is not something anyone can control except oneself. And ignore that you don't see things the same way they do. I am not judging anyone; I am just giving you my thoughts and something to remember when you make close contact with this kind of person. So please try to be happy in front of people, especially those who dislike you. It kills them more to see you are so glad when all they want is to make you unhappy. I am saying try not to get even as we all die eventually. Death is the ultimate freedom. But you cannot take your own life. You are not allowed to do that, so you will go where you are supposed to go after death. You have to live this life that has been given to you. Because it is your life, your future, and the present belong only to you.

Chapter 3

African Supreme

There are good men in this world, especially in Africa. Trust me. If you are a tourist or just visiting, they will help you when you are lost. Back then, we did not have GPS or Google Maps in my time. People often relied on each other for information and directions for where they were going. People often got lost because of limited transportation sources. I come from the sun. That is how I see myself, from a land that is so hot. If you stand out too long in the sun, the soles of your shoes start to melt. Mother Nature often sends clouds to blind the sun now and then. And this helps me cool off from the sun's hotness.

There is a mountain in my homeland; Aza it is called. It is not too far from the city. There are waterfalls from the top of the hills and freshwater. The layers of the mountains are so thin that when you run on the mountain's surface, you can hear the echo from the bottom. You can only bike or walk up the hill. You can listen to the sound of the waterfalls from a distance. I want to build a city there one day called Sun City. It will be an African paradise, a place for everyone.

The city will be a place with rules that protect everyone, not just the rich. There will also be a maximum number of people allowed to live there first. As the city continues to develop, more residents will be accepted. Mushroom homes will be built there, too; I designed them myself. These mushroom homes will have elevators stretching from the bottom six hundred feet to the sky. They will angle each other and be connected with stairs, about thirty millimeters in thickness. The base is a playing field with tunnels going underground. The mushroom houses will be hooked like three skyscrapers standing close together, forming a triangle. At every intersection between the buildings will be a shopping mall, a restaurant, a barbershop, and grocery stores. The plans call for many trees and playgrounds.

Sun City will give us a second chance to make Africa great again. During the era of slavery, we lost almost half our ways and dignity. Africans have ruled the earth from the beginning; everyone knows that. That is one of the reasons I was born, to put the thing back in order. It is time to take back what belongs to us and put the world back in the right direction as we did in the beginning.

In my research, 80 percent of the African countries have been battling with limited energy sources over the years. That includes Nigeria. There is energy everywhere, including in the sun and the wind. We have to find a way to harvest it. Without solid, reliable sources of electricity, my dream of building Sun City is nothing but a dream. We need a new source of energy to help boost the African continent out of poverty and create a better community that can help everyone, especially those in West Africa. The West African energy pool needs renovation. It needs to be upgraded to power the surrounding areas with energy everyone can afford without sharing or rationing. You will have constant lights and enough energy for the city and factories to attract investors. No government can create a job without foreign investors, so you need to create a risk-free environment for investors to invest. I hope to figure out how to build a portable energy source that can generate electricity by itself one day. That is the only thing that has never been invented and is the way to go now. I know it will benefit the world, and my homeland will reap the best rewards. This will boost the Nigerian and Canadian economies as they will access the products and services.

Hypothetically, are you imagining how to achieve this device? I will need an electrical power unit to help generate and regenerate power. The machine will recirculate and stabilize voltage by itself. I will need a two-millimeter-long small power source with blades to create a faster copper electromagnet. I will also need jet fuel in first grade. It should not be more than thirty pounds. You will build twenty-seven of these devices attached using the same coil. That's where the energy will be gathered together. This allows the purest of the points to stack in one place, and an electrical insert will provide the energy boom. This enables a self-sustainable energy source. Three years of sustainable energy will be guaranteed if this can be built. It is a new product and still needs to be researched and developed. But this is doable for the future, creating energy that can last forever, like the stars in the sky. Imagine if you could capture lightning and compress it in one cone. You would have unlimited energy. That's the idea.

On this planet, life is more complicated than you think. The system is doing the best it can. Some ignorant people overshadow the rule of law, which causes other countries to suffer more than they deserve. This is what we know as chaos. And it will not stop until we stand together and say, "Enough is enough." I am part of the generation that must make everything all right because we are the ones that have been given authority to make changes for a better world for humankind from the origin of the stars. I am going to involve God in this. To be clear, it is not my place to question what you believe, but I hope you believe in God. Having said that, if you believe in God, may he bless you. After all, salvation is personal.

Everyone believes and thinks differently. I can only tell you that I am here to help humankind. I'm not here to destroy anything or scare you with what I see in the dream world.

I have four mothers. My biological mom gave birth to me; others joined hands to raise me. Mother Agnes was one of the kindest of them all. My real mom is always busy working, and the rest take turns helping with the teachings of the things to come. Mama Agnes was the one who truly knew who I would be, who I am. She predicted my arrival a year before my mother conceived me. What I'm trying to say is may her soul rest in peace. Hopefully, I can complete the work I came here to do in her memory one day.

Everyone, even the kids in school, knew who I was or what I would be. They were scared of my dad and mom, though I did not know why. I was not supposed to play with them; I was not even supposed to have a sleepover as much as I wanted to. It was not a palace rule. You see, the palace has rules. Playing was not for me, nor was it for my father or grandfather. You could play on the court with other kids, but someone always had to go with you if you were going out. I wanted to go outside. My father did not mind, but my mother did not want me to go anywhere.

My mother always wanted to control me. She wanted to be the only person I listened to. And she was the only one who cared about me. She gave me so many gifts. She worked hard and always supported me, even though we always fought. She always bragged about all the things she did for me. I would tell her, "I did not ask you to do any of that. You did it alone, and now you rub it in my face."

But in the end, she is the most beautiful mother, and I have made her proud; her son was the first to leave the village on his own. Despite her being fearful, she still trusted me and believed in me.

It also makes her proud that people want to follow in my footsteps. They do not have the same kingship as we do. We rule them and tell them what to do. Even when they die, their dead bodies must be brought to us to say goodbye. Most of the time, I see their spirits walking through the front of the palace, and I scream to my mother and father, "This man who is sick is here in the palace."

My father will come out of his bedroom in the palace, look around, and say to me, "Udejii [meaning the one born in the harvest]. I did not see anything."

"Father, I saw them," I reply.

He will smile, but I can see sadness at the same time. And he will say to me, "It's OK. They are passing to go back from where they were created." I was the only family member who could see the dead come back to us after they died. My father knew why I could see them before they died or were buried. Most of the time, they could see me too.

The villagers knew me as the bringer of light, food, and water from time to time. Nobody could deny who I was in the village. Some called me *ogbanje,* meaning spirit child, or in between. They knew who I was from the prophecy of old Mother Agnes from childhood, who had predicted my coming to the family. I was to help everyone. As a child, I often wondered, how am I going to help everyone while still living with my mother, and she is the one who makes all my decisions?

I could see how happy the villagers were each time I returned from the city where I lived with some family members. When they saw me, they hugged me and asked how I was doing. Was I OK? Was I sick? I would say, "No, I am fine." I could hear them whisper, "He is ogbanje."

You cannot live, nor can you die. I can see the living and the dead. I knew who I was, and as I got older, everything began to disappear slowly because the real world is a hard place. I want to put this in good order so that you understand my meaning. To be a hero is not easy when everyone depends on and counts on you.

I have access to both the dream and the real world. Very soon, I will tell you about the dream world. I must explain all this to know where I am coming from. But for now, I will stick to the real world and serve humans better. Part of me is human. The other part I will explain to you when the time is right. But I am human. It is arrogant

27

not to answer straight questions or hide the truth. That's enough—no more hiding. Let's move forward.

We have to recognize that humans come first. Humans are like children. Like my children, they come first. No matter what happens in the universe, humans will always exist. And Nigeria is my homeland, and a part of me belongs there. We must acknowledge the pain of those broken hearts. It does not matter if they are right or wrong; their hearts are broken. It is not karma; I do not do karma. I base my judgments on the information I have. Humans often contradict me, which brings us to the purest state of mind. The more refined you are, the more you can categorize everything between the natural and dream worlds.

I previously mentioned that I wanted to build a self-sustainable energy source. I also have the idea of space homes and how they might be possible to invent. I will explain more about space homes in a later chapter. But for now, let's move to the next phase.

The last time we talked about the dream and the real world, I did not explain as much as possible. Life is tough, and there is nothing we can do about it unless we unite to conquer poverty. To be successful in life, you have to manage risks. To be honest, you must keep thriving no matter what happens, even if it sometimes seems you have hit rock bottom. But that is not true. Do not listen to the voice telling you to give up. If you do not, you can never achieve your potential. Don't listen to it. There is a light within you. Even though you may fail, keep going and do not stop. Keep learning about everything you come across in this world. You do not have to explain anything to anyone about what you have learned but apply the skills you have learned if needed. All this awareness will transcend you to a higher state of mind and knowledge. It does not matter if you know it all or not. It is called self-confidence. To understand yourself, you must acknowledge your abilities. Then the rest will fall in line.

Chapter 4

My Dreams

Before I start explaining my dreams in detail, one thing you should know is the fact and my opinion. We must separate the dream world from the real world. A world you can see is not the same as the one you cannot see or control, even though it might seem real. Why do we have to do that? We must acknowledge this so that those who read this book understand its purpose. This book is a message, not random words. It contains all the ideas and meanings of life before and after.

The universe is connected in one extensive network. As humans, we must separate the things we can touch and feel in this world and the things we dream about, which is another world. The same reality, the same plane, has the same consequences. The only difference between this world and the dream world is the advantage of flying in dreams and the unlimited power of freeing yourself from this broken world, where lovers kill each other, families steal from one another, and countries lie to other countries to distract them from paying attention to their belongings. That is the difference between here and there. Freedom in the dream world is unlimited. But in the real world, we have intersections, and because of those intersections, we have laws, rules, and boundaries that reduce our access to be utterly free, like in the dream world.

I am going to take you back to where it all started. I was young, scared, and only thirteen years old. I got a new pair of shoes from my mom. That was the first time I had flown out in the universe. Why do I remember the shoes my mother gave me as a gift? Because it symbolized the beginning of it all. That night in my dreams, I lifted into the sky. From there, I could see my shoes on the floor. It was the first time I had flown and probably one of the scariest moments in my life. It lasted about eight hours in the dream world. But here in the real world, it was only like an hour. During those eight hours, I was scared and ran. Men carrying swords and horsewhips arose from the ground. They were chasing me, shouting, "Kill him!" They were so close.

Suddenly, wings sprung from my back, and I lifted into the sky. That was the scariest moment in my life. The men started throwing swords and spears into the atmosphere. With speed, I moved. I was already in space and could see the spears. Some had guns, and I could see gunfire. I flew faster and faster into space. I saw the spears falling on the ground as I lifted into the sky and flew far above the heavens. I did not know what it meant at that time. I was just scared.

I was afraid because I did not know where I was going or how long I would fly. *Am* I going to fall at some point? I wondered. But I just kept flapping my wings. I could maneuver my speed; I was totally in control of my speed.

After I reached far into space, I stood there for a couple of seconds. I looked around to see if anyone or anything was there. Nothing. Just dark blue with stars all over the place. I started to dive down to the earth at the same speed. I landed on a cashew farm with lots of cashews. There were also mangos. I ate some and then flew home. When I awoke, I felt like I was still flying, my head full of wonders. The simplest way to explain it is to look up in the sky for fifteen seconds. Then look down on earth, and you can see the difference. The ground will feel like a garbage bin.

That morning I couldn't find my shoes. I wondered, where are my new shoes, the ones my mother bought me? They were not there. The shoes later appeared somewhere at home. Two days later, a friend came to my house and asked to borrow some shoes because he had a date. I had just met this guy, so he was not that close of a friend. But I gave him my brand-new shoes. I never got them back. The next day I left the country.

Translating the dream world to the real world can be right or wrong. But the most crucial part is that you make the decisions. You can bring it to reality, or you can choose not to. That is how I translated it then, the shoes, the flight, the people trying to kill me when I began flying for the first time. In the real world, I have a friend asking me for shoes. The shoes were the only pattern and connection I could find in this dream world. They were the only things that existed in both worlds.

One night, I learned how to flap my wings as I flew across the ocean. I never knew fear until that day. Do you know fear? It was scary for a person who did not know how to swim. I was flying so low across the ocean, as low as 150 feet, so close to the sea. All I could think about was falling. But one thing was sure. My wings were strong.

I kept gazing at my shadows and reflection on the ocean's surface, looking for a city or anything that could get me off the sea. I finally found land. There were glasshouses everywhere, all attached, I tried to land, but I could not land on the glass because of its slip lee. So, I had to find ground to land on.

When I landed, I could hear my wings scraping the surface floor, like the sound of wind echoing. I could listen to the sound of my foot hopping on the floor. Its echo was like a lion's roar. But finally, I was on the ground at last.

Oh, there is something I forgot to mention. While I was flying across the ocean, there came a time when I began to enjoy the flight. I decided to look at my reflection in the sea. I couldn't see my face clearly, but I was five times taller and more extensive than in real life. That was the first time I saw my wings, their size, and how I looked with them on. I was wearing this white cloth; my father had a similar one long ago. The white cloth waved behind me like a cape. It looked oversized to me. It was impressive. I was elated. In that case, I believed that having wings was not a bad thing. You were considered a witch from where I came from if you had wings. All of this was part of my fear. But in the real world, I was not a bad person. The way I flew was not the same as how witches flew. I learned all this by myself; nobody taught me anything. That is when I began to embrace my gift. I started searching for an answer as to whether it meant something in this real world. As a teenager, anything was possible for me. My mind was wild.

As an African boy, I knew more than most people my age. But I often wondered how this affects or improves my real life, I began to study it, but for many years, my translation was inaccurate; it did not even come close to what I felt was the interpretation of the real world and dream world; on my first flight, there was a pattern, which was the shoe. And the landing was completely different.

When I flew across the ocean, in the real world, I was in an unknown place; the phrase I use to describe it is the spirit world." Here on this planet, the people there are considered the opposite of humanity even though they're human like everyone else. But it is also where angels come to live because of the evil done by the wicked. The angels are forced to intervene.

But it is still like the spirit world to me. In this place, the people have something they believe in, a different understanding and mindset that allows the natural ways and things to be forgotten. They have forgotten what it means to humans. However, some still remember that we are all connected in different ways. Others deviate from the truth and invent their own, including the teaching and meaning of existence and life itself. They go beyond what we know as a human right; no one should go there. I lost something there, something vital. Anyway, we have new memories now. That is how the dream world works.

Chapter 5

Dream Awareness

There is a window to understanding that you are dreaming in dream awareness, and you know you are dreaming. When I first experienced this, I was overwhelmed. It was like I was awake but still sleeping. My eyes were wide open, and I could see I was awake. I froze my body to keep it from moving. I didn't want to wake myself up.

That's when I started to collect information from the dream world. Let me share with you the night I saw the heaven gate. I was flying low on a gravel road, maybe fifteen feet above the ground, when I heard men singing and machines crewing. I listened to the older woman's voice, saying from a distance, hide. If you see them, they will see you. I decided to hide in the bush, not far from the road. Why? I do not know, but I wondered, why am I hiding?

Then the woman said, "Hide. The enemy is coming! If you see them, they will see you." She said it over and over until it faded away from my ear. And they all passed by. There was so much noise, like an army and machines. I could hear the sound and felt like I was watching their movements. I crawled out from the bush; I was so scared. I had seen fear before, but that was the worst fear I felt. I was grateful when it was all said and done. It's in the past now.

One of my hopes in life is to help the world. If I can't help, I pray that someone will help. Poverty is a disease that kills more people than any disease on the earth.

Let's continue; I heard the older woman's voice again after the enemies and their machines passed by. I lifted into the sky. It was the first time I saw the gates of the heavens. A beauty, I call it. I flew closer, and the beauty could blind my eyes. I kept flying closer; it seemed like I passed in slow motion. Time seemed frozen. There I was, in control. I took my time looking closely at every inch of the gate. Its gate stretched across space and time. It was decorated with tiny lights, like Christmas lights, from one end of the space to the other. It was pure blue, made with diamonds, hearts—like the symbol of love—crosses, and stars, all beautiful. It was a scene of extraordinary beauty.

I have seen heaven and earth split into two parts in flying dreams, one side in the plain sky. There were no stars. It was like daytime in the real world, but smoky-white and the other just blue, with no stars. I ask myself where all the stars are. Where did they go? I woke up. I looked through my window; I saw many people outside shooting the star.

Imagine the space between Planet Earth and the moon. I gave it the name Outer Planet. It's not the same as the outer universe. I've been there. There is a triangle window inside the over-circle. Inside that window was a door to the external universe; I flew closer, figuring out its purpose. The over-circle is attached to the very end of our universe. I say to myself, Let's go find out what it is. I opened the over-circle, which looked like a small planet, and went inside a triangle; there was a door in the center of the triangle, just like in the outer universe. I opened the door and went through; I came out the other side and was dark, empty, and full of blackness. There was black smoke everywhere. I didn't waste one second staying there. I knew it was the wrong place. A place I dared not enter. I turned back and shut the door. All of this was in the dream world.

Dream awareness is like when I'm half asleep and half awake; it is not the same as when I woke up and remember my dreams; it is like it's happening in the real world. One night, I was summoned to a planet I had never been to before; it was the first time I discovered that planets are alive, and they all have their creators. On this planet, the creator is a woman, and she has a daughter, and she is so angry with the mother; the daughter wants to destroy the world, she has been mad at her for a long time, for many years, she has never seen seeing her, I guess that's why she was mad at her. When I came to the planet, I saw the daughter in a dark dress. Her whole body was covered in black mud gashed down like raindrops; I was standing beside a lake right in front of me with a small brown dog, and she looked at me and said you are the one they sent? You can't stop me; when she was about to destroy everything, the mom emerged from the lake and shouted stop. The said daughter, where have you been? I have a daughter now I will love her more than you love me, the mom said I love you; they start talking to each other the mom said if you destroy the world everything dies, then she looked at me and said write what happens here down and return it your world. And then they embraced each other and made peace. Then I return to earth, which is part of the reason I'm writing this book.

Two days before Christmas, I was flying as always in the dream world, but here on Earth, I decided to search for Atlantis, the famous lost city of ancient times. That will be a significant discovery if I can pinpoint the exact location; I searched every inch of the oceans, but I couldn't find any lost city. And remember, deserts used to be the ocean. I fly again to the deserts I can see; there is no lost city anywhere; in my thought, I said maybe it doesn't exist, or the universe doesn't want this generation to find it; somehow universe knows I'm searching for Atlantis, five days later I travel back in time, this time I wasn't flying, I end up in Egypt, two thousand years that day to be exact there was a war between humans and something else, far worst greater than humans, I couldn't see what was killing them clearly, but I can see people screaming, running. I saw the pyramids standing tall, shining. That's how I knew I was in Egypt; in between pyramids, there was a temple; I saw the elders talking, whispering in each other ears, one look directly. I hear them discussing how they are losing the war; these ancients have technologies I have never seen before; the elders decided to need new technology or weapon that could prevent the invaders from seeing them. If you can't see them, you can't kill them. Hide technology or hide machine. So, they invented the device to hide humans from their killers. The device works in a group of people, but in thousands, I saw them gather everyone together in place. Then they brought this thing that looked like a gas lamp but in three stands, and turned on, in a couple of seconds the whole people disappeared except the elders that were operating it, then ask one of the elders where do they go? did you beam them to another place? He said no, there are here with us; we can't see them, so does the enemy, and now they are free to live their life happily; when the war ends, we will use the same device and bring them back. Moreover, the war continued to the extent that the device was destroyed, trapping everyone that was hidden on the other side forever. In our world, in this reality, you will see from time-to-time specific energy will appear, on the road, at home, and even in public places; these are particles flowing from the hidden world to our world. Sometimes, people say I just had a Déjà vu; that's the connection that pass-through from the secret world not too far from ours; even sometimes, I find myself in some places I knew I had been before. This world is attached to another world hidden from human eyes but co-exists on the same planet but in a different reality. Sooner or later, it will separate into two different dimensions; my advice to you is to keep your mind positive at all times; no one knows when the final process will be complete.

Dreams can be scary. I ask myself why all these dreams about planets and earth, something or someone is trying to destroy us, and the world is not paying attention. Today just passed out on my couch. Here we are again. I saw another kind of machine. At first, I thought it was a paper plane; then it transformed into another type of machine dripping some chemical like raindrops peeling people's skin off; it changes as it flies and disappears into the cloud.

In another episode, the musician P-Q, an Afrobeat singer, and I and one other girl, I don't know her name, went back to the past from Africa we went to in England in 1717 we used the boat on the water when getting in England the people they were so fat their hair is different the climate is dusty and smell of oil. He is singing, and the girl is dancing with people who have never heard of the song. They were amazed and happy; suddenly, he stopped singing. I asked him why do you stop singing. He said the time was not moving here; it was freezing; he could not sing because the time was too far away, and he was not even born yet; then I woke up. Sometimes I wonder how you determine what is real and what isn't. the next night, I just woke up; I didn't dream. It was peaceful last night. The fact the dream word exists, and when you wake up, this reality exists as well, and when you are dreaming is another reality which has nothing to do with this reality, but they are connected in some ways; I just went to bed early, and I woke up eleven pm, I went another place it's like here, police are there was an accident two trucks collide with each other block the whole high way I have to detour on the detour there is another intersection there is the police with a different kind of motorcycle that carry people but has two wheels with a hydraulic pump like a parachute when it stops the pump will push the ground holding both. They are driving maybe twenty feet above the bottom. One person rides the other person checks the cars; it has different kinds of sounds of silence. In another intersection ahead, a woman is crossing with a child; however, on the left side of the meeting, construction is going on; I see the roller the equipment that the pavements on the road, the same as here the color yellow, and the same vest construction worker's wear, the same road signs left turns right turns. How do we determine what is real? I don't know, ladies and gentlemen, I don't know, but what I do know is that my dream felt so real. The things I dream about, the things I see in my dreams, are overwhelming; sometimes, I don't think I know what is real anymore. Flying dreams, yes, I remember I must hurry up and do what I came to do before I woke up. This is another level of dreaming; I work like everybody else in the real world, and I never remember the city I live in in the real world. My dreams were so real and transparent as they were real until I woke up. How do you know what is real and what isn't? I might be dreaming right now, is everyone dreaming right now? Is all humanity dreaming right now? There is a possibility that everyone is dreaming right now; all this happening today could be one mass dreaming, sleeping somewhere, which might explain why no one knows where we come from and who we are. Or the ultimate question are we alone? I think the universe wanted us to see and understand night and day; the representation of the images we see in the dream world is inserted human mind, brain, and spirit. To thoroughly see the universe's beauty and splendors accompanying the daylight after the night sky. No one truly dies, we move from one world to another, and we are in that dream world if, as the person wakes, the other planet will no longer exist but only in your mind. Imagine, if I am right, hepatically, this is what is happening. Then who is in control?

In the previous chapter, I mentioned a baby and the mother; let me explain it better. One night I was invited to the cities of gods somewhere in this universe; when I arrived at the temple, I could still feel the overwhelming echoing on my mind and body right now. Anyway, proceeding to what happened that night. When I entered the temple, I looked towards the ceiling; I saw two planets facing each other one planet is earth, the other is an ice planet, and yet it is not cold. The water in the temple is a stream flowing on the stone upward instead of downward; I was thirsty for water; I wanted to drink the water, but I was scared something might happen to me;

I had never seen any stream that flowed upward. The child and the ship traveling away land, the mother is pregnant, she has been deceived by a group of men, who plans to kill her and the baby, but she thought they were taking her somewhere while I'm in the temple I had a vision they were going to kill her and the baby and eat them, they want the power that is in the child. I saw the sun start acting out, like breaking apart, because the child is born in another land, the child must return to temples, or the world will come to an end; I can see the sun recover as I told stories to the gods of what will happen if the child is born another land, they sent men in a brown horse to retrieve the child and the mother and bring them back to the temple, I turn around and went up I can see the two planets so close to each other, the feelings make hair body tingle like a goosebump as I walk around the temple, I can hear the gods angrily exchange words, saying unless the child returns the temple they are doomed. I don't know what will happen to the child, but I believe the child will return to the temple. The life of the entire planet depends on it. There is a visitor from another land, a god. He was sitting with the gods when the story broke out; he was so mad hid disappeared when I went upstream; I believe he went after the child to save them. I am still wandering around; the whole place is made of stones, water flowing every Conor of the temple; the water scares me. I see the two planets breaking into each other; the temple is checking like an earthquake, of the god, said the child is too far away. If the child is not back soon, everything will be lost. Then, the two-man in horses ran at high speed to reach the child before the temple collapsed. Then I was sitting on the bench made of stone, and there was another person there. I could not see his face clearly and was still thirsty for water; I didn't want to drink the water from the temple; I had this weird feeling that something terrible might happen. While I was still sitting on the bench thinking of water to drink, the gods that disappeared in search of the child reappeared carrying a pregnant woman almost dead, barely breathing; I looked up. The sun is back to normal; the two planets restore the gods' balance as all is in order. Then I left the temple and headed back to earth; at this point, I am convinced the mother and her child were ok.

I woke up from Easter Saturday to Sunday morning and fell asleep again at three am. I found myself wandering in a place I had never been there before; lots of people everywhere, black people but not like black people on earth; they were short but beautiful, and the color of their skin was so shiny, like black and blue metallic, there is these family a mother and her two girls her youngest daughter was adorable, her skin is so polished like a diamond dark blue her eyes were so white, you will want to kiss her skin. I tell her and her mom you are beautiful; why is your skin so beautifully made this way? She just smiled and then went away.

I start asking people where I am. Nobody wanted to say a thing. Finally, one of the men walking around said to me look for the elders. Did I reply which elders? Where are they? On his side of the stomach, there's a scare. I look around; all the men have scared on the side of their stomachs; I ask, what is that? What happened to you? He said to seek the elders.

I started going around looking for the elders. Finally, I found elders sitting around this stone table like a ritual ceremony; I asked, "Are you, elders? They all raised their heads toward me and started mumbling, and one of them said to me you think you can destroy us? I said what? No, I want to know where I am to find my way home. Then the woman and her two kids were standing beside me; I asked one of the daughters where is your father? she said all the men were castrated, and the elders took out testicles; I replied why? She said they could control everyone, they do have sex, but they can't make babies, and the elders create everyone; I ask the elders why they would do such a horrible thing, and they reply in an aggressive voice, this is our way of life, do not question our authority, I said this is wrong, you must stop such practice, then of the elders told me the only way stop it is to compete with one of the leaders, in jumping. Jumping where? The young girl pointed out toward rang like a river so deep you can't see the bottom, said you have to jump from here across to the other side if you win, they will stop the practice of castration, and if you lose, the method will go on.

This is half a kilometer across; how am I supposed to jump that? I thought to myself, this was impossible. Then I remembered I had a wing and asked whether I could fly. No, they said you could only jump. Then everyone started gathering around; one of the leaders among the elders made the first jump and failed; I thought to myself, if the powerful elder had fallen, I stand no chance; the little girl looked at me and said believe in yourself, and you can do impossible things. So, I jumped, made it across, was excited to save men from castration, and flew back. Everyone was happy. I saw all the elders dissolve on the ground like snow and heat. Then I woke up.

Chapter 6

My Flying Dreams in The Dream World

The first time I was transported to the dream world, I was not a child anymore. My transition from the real world to the dream world was something new. I had never seen myself without a body before. How did I know I transported my body?

One night there was one thing different from other dreams. When I lifted into the sky, I had to open my window from the third floor of my apartment, and then I flew. When I looked back to my bed, there was no one there, nobody, no me, no one. I kept wondering, Am I dead? Where is my body? I was a little worried. My main concern was what would happen when I came back. There is nobody to return to.

I flew on, trying not to think about it. This was probably a double-deep experience. I ended up looking for the same crystal stone in the corner of the universe. When the time came to return to earth, I flew away and ended up in a forest. There were significant and tall trees, some almost three hundred feet tall, Some taller than the seventh-story building; on the base floor, there was no grass, only dry leaves accumulated over time. I asked myself, "How did I end up here? Is it because I have nobody? I have to find a way to fly out. I still have wings; I just need space to fly out." I started walking, searching for open spaces. But there was not enough room for me to fly out as there were too many trees everywhere. I kept walking, looking for a hole in the sky between the trees to fly out. I could hear my feet as I walked on the dry leaves, making a crunchy noise beneath my feet. There was no one else around.

The trees stretched for thousands of kilometers; there seemed no end. There was no shade, no slope: just trees, big giant trees. I wasn't afraid since I had my body with me. But then I wondered if I would ever get out of there. Then I remembered something from my childhood in Africa. Whenever there was a festival in my grandmother's village, we would go hunting. There were always dry leaves in the forest. We played under the trees with the dry leaves that fell on the ground. I thought, just pretend you are playing with leaves, and that kept me going.

I walked for many days. I almost give up. And thanks to God, the dream world has no boundaries. You don't get hungry. I could be there for many years without getting hungry unless I came across a fruit. Or a town where someone was getting married. Then you could eat and drink. And within a second, you would be back where you used to be. I call those events passages of time because they usually appeared from nowhere and disappeared in the blink of an eye.

It took me two weeks of walking in the forest before I found a place from which I thought I could fly out. That was two weeks in the dream world for one night in the real world. It wasn't enough, but it was something. I tried to get out, but I couldn't. My wings were too long. They got stuck in these soft coil plants, like a shrink wrap. I spent almost forty-five minutes there until finally, I pulled away from the plants and lifted to the sky.

It was beautiful, though it was just an empty sky, no blue sky, no stars. I went back to space. I didn't even care to go home anymore. And that's where I saw Jesus Christ with a sword in his hands; he was not a black man or white; he wore a silver coat stretched to his feet. It was attached to the sky from where he stood on a cloud. He kept pointing his sword to the four corners of the universe, one at a time. He did this over and over again.

Then an older woman's voice came to me; she said, "That is where Jesus controls the four corners of the world. If he ever stops, the world will fall apart." Then she and I started flying side by side; it was the first time I flew so close to her that I could almost touch her dress as we continued the journey. Though we flew close together, each time I opened my eyes to look at her, there was a force like heavy wind, keeping my head in the other direction so that I wouldn't see her face.

Then the older woman took me to hell. "Never set your foot here, no matter what; don't you ever come close to this place. Do not fly across the ridge or the quadrant," she warned. We were about a kilometer away, looking at hell from a distance. It was so red. We could see blazing flames of lava coming out.

We continued flying. We flew far into space, into deep space. Then we saw the stars coiled together like a C curved like a big trumpet, with different color stars attached to them. They were beautiful, I wanted to touch them, but she slapped my hand and told me not to touch them. I stood there for a while, looking at the beauty. We left and kept flying the last I saw was a dragon-like cloud; I was trying to figure it was alive or just a shadow, then the older woman had gone, so I left for the earth.

As I traveled back to earth, I stopped in the in-between space. I looked at the four corners. I stood there for a brief moment. I could walk around there usually like walking around a park yet is in the space. I stood there. I looked around, and there was nothing. I searched for the crystal stone; there was no stone, then I returned to earth.

I usually sleep face up. I don't know for sure if that plays a vital role in my dreams in the dream world; it would make sense if it did. But If I slept sideways, my arm would be stuck under me; I wouldn't be able to fly. I would only be able to fly sideways, which is challenging, and eventually, I would fall. I need to lift my arms to be able to raise my wings.

One beautiful night I was flying in this space. I saw the moon, maybe like thirty half-moons. They were in circles, weaved around like wool, overlapping each other. In the center were three rails of stars, one going one way and the other going the opposite direction, three rings of stars with different colors, and the half-moon weaving around stars like a shield; the moon was going the other way. One on top of the other. I looked at the stars. They were different colors, beautiful. I searched for a gap between the moon and the stars, and there was no gap. Everything looked perfect. It was a unique design of beauty in the open space. So, I moved on.

I next went to Mars, the planet that is famous to everyone. It's my favorite planet. It's close to home. I feel a little cold but not as much; I wonder why the sun is too far from Mars. Not like on earth, where the sun is so much closer, and the sun is so tiny. I look down at my feet. It's just red soil, just like in Africa. I looked around. Everywhere was so familiar to me; in my thought, I knew I had been here many times. Do you know how they say there are no living things on Mars? Well, I can tell you otherwise. There are people there, but they don't have the same technology as ours; they are humans like us but more petite; I saw them coming out from the ground like a cave but like US off-limit army base underground doors. And we were cheering with me, smiling like everyone was happy I was back, the same as people on earth, when you went away so many years and came back everyone will come and say hi, it was a good feeling. If we decide that the north of Mars will be the same as earth, this village will be in the northwest of Mars; It's there; I've seen it in a dream world. I have eaten with them. They are humans like us. They act like us; they build their houses like ours but on the ground, they talk like us. When I saw them, we were speaking the same language. They understood me, and I understood them. I spent time with them; then I flew away.

Many nights I can choose where to go. But sometimes, I am not in control of where I am going; it is like being summoned. I dislike being controlled, but I respect the older woman's wishes. For some reason, she is like a guardian.

Those nights when I can choose where I want to go, I always select Mars and Saturn; they are my favorite planets. I like Mars because I like interacting with the indigenous people of Mars. I chose Saturn because it allows me to see its true nature from a distance, but not too far away. Saturn is a beautiful planet. To see Saturn correctly, you need to sit on one of the stones of Saturn's rings. And float around with it and can see everything. I have to fly around it some night, just flying in a circle looking at the true master of all planets. Some nights I sit in and gaze upon the universe and its beauty.

All I ever wanted was to share my experiences with the world; I hope I bring you comfort and a good night's sleep.

There's another planet that has no name. There are lots like it in the universe. I have to fly around to see it. That day after I finished on Mars, I went home. I woke up, took a shower, and went to work like everyone else.

Another night was different. I was summoned. I didn't choose to go there. When we arrived, I discovered it was not a planet. It was a city in space. At the bottom of the city, I could see a cloud holding it up. The whole town was made of dark-brown glass stretching hundreds of kilometers away.

When I arrived, the older woman was already there. "Can you believe all the adventures, training, and traveling we have shared?" the old woman asked.

"Yes. I reply, an experience I will never forget." That was the first time I saw her face. Previously I only heard her voice and the sound of her wings flapping beside me. I never cared to look. Besides, there was always something obscuring her face when I tried looking at her. And there was no point in trying to know who she was; it was like I knew who she was.

Then we both flew to a town in the same city; when we arrived, Barack Obama was there. This was before he became president of the United States. I didn't know who he was back then. Samuel L. Jackson was there, my father was there, and Jesus Christ was there. Those were the only people I recognized. And elders are sitting on the upper level; their chair is made of gray stones; I can't see their faces.

They concluded that Barack would become president. Years later, when I saw him as a US presidential candidate on TV, I told my friend he would win. My friend said, "No, he will not. They will kill him before he makes it to the White House." I again told him Obama would win. And two years later, he became president of the United States. I am not trying to interpret the dream world as the real world. But when I am summoned, it is for an important reason. But what I could not understand was why me? Here on earth, I'm no one. I couldn't find any tangible reason they would include me in that meeting.

After it was decided that Barack Obama would become president, I left. The older woman didn't come with me. I flew into space. Sometimes I flew on my back, like swimming backstroke. I could feel the cold wind on my skin. When I got close to the earth, I stopped. I love to look at the planet from a distance when it is about the size of a soccer ball. I carried it in my hands. I opened it with two hands, like when you opened a shrink-wrapped gift. I looked at the world map and chose where to go. I would either go to Africa or back to Canada.

When I returned to earth, I usually went to Africa to see my mother. I would sit on the roof of my building in my village and watch her, but she couldn't see me. Then I traveled across the ocean back to Canada; I was home within a few seconds. The speed is phenomenal. The pace has to do with time because I can spend two weeks in a dream world in one night. Three weeks in one night, even double dip, double dive, and triple dive in one night. That is why time is fast for me.

Double dip is when I dream, wake up in the dream world, sleep again in the dream world, and dream again. Please, this is not *Inception*, and I am not Leonardo DiCaprio. It's not the same. The triple dip is when I dream, wake up, dream again, and remember all the dreams when I wake up. And when I wake up, I am exhausted. It can take thirty minutes for me to move my hands. The dream world is like another world, though similar to ours. If we find a way to have any conscious mind cross over to the dream world and come back at the time of their choosing, that would be something, wouldn't it? Then we all will have a place to escape reality. Instead of the alternative of mending breaking hearts, we travel to the dream world. We can escape the realities in this world.

Chapter 7

The War in My Dream World

People or something are always trying to help this world and everything in it. This is especially with the sun. The sun is essential to us, but it is also dangerous. It has shown me the bad side of it. One night I lifted into space as usual. I wasn't summoned; this was just me, parading across the solar system. Then I flew too close to the sun. That was the first time I saw the solar flare. I could see the sun spilling flares everywhere. It didn't hurt me, of course. I saw the flare travel through all the planets, including earth in its middle. The blaze destroyed everything in its path. I could hear people screaming and crying.

I flew back to earth as fast as I could. Many people all over the world were burned. Cities were destroyed. That was the first time I was afraid of my dreams. I never had war in my dreams. I made decisions in my dreams, saw beautiful stars, flap my wings. That's all I did. I did not participate in wars. But in this war, I tried to help as much as possible. But half the population was devastated. It went on for almost a year—war and war and war and war. This solar flare was just one scenario.

In another scenario on another night, I was shown another possibility of a coming war, this one in a different form. I don't know what aliens are, but I believe they are like people, like us. Another night I flew into the sky, as always, in space. Sometimes I stayed in the earth's atmosphere, and that say didn't go into space. I just flew into the sky. I could see people moving and going about their business. That night I opened my window. I was planning to take my body with me and transport it. I do that sometimes. As mentioned in the previous chapters, I always look back at my bed when I lift to ensure I'm not dead. As long as there is nobody, I'm good.

When I opened my window and looked outside, the world was destroyed. Building's skyscrapers were broken into pieces. Most adults were dead. Children everywhere were looking for food. When I went outside, I cried, "No, no!"

The children were so happy they could see me. They ran up to me, saying, "Look at the star. Look at the star."

I flew away in search of survivors. The only people I could see were the children. I flew into the space to look for the older woman. I wanted to ask her why my world was destroyed. If they planned to destroy Planet Earth, I would have been summoned. I would have been part of the decision or had an idea of what would come. I needed answers, but she was nowhere to be found. So, I returned to earth and tried to help as many children as possible.

In another scenario, it was some people or species. As I said previously, I don't believe in aliens, but if they exist, they are just other beings like us. They have a planet as we do. They have families and technology as we do. But for some reason, they want to destroy us. I said they would fail; they had tried so many times in that dream. This attempt lasted approximately six to eight months of the vision of our planet getting destroyed; every night, the same dream, I didn't want to sleep anymore. I was so scared; one night in the real world, I prayed for a sign of what I must do to prevent the earth from being destroyed. I went to sleep after my prayer, the same dream I tried to fight back, but I failed.

However, they came up with this devious idea of melting off our space station materials and combining them with some of their materials to form a hot mold of about three hundred degrees of melted iron. Using our space station, they would transport the dissolved iron to earth and spray it like a helicopter spraying fire extinguisher in a forest fire. And when it fell on your skin, it burned it off and melted you to ashes. It kills thousands, and thousands of people perish.

I lost it after that. I didn't want to go to sleep anymore. I didn't want to dream anymore. I tried to tell my partner, but I was that worried about scaring her, or I didn't exactly know how she would react and process all that, and this is a girl who doesn't dream. I didn't bother telling her.

The dreams weren't fun anymore. It was not right anymore. I was angry in both the real and the dream worlds. I was looking for a solution to the problem.

But one thing always remained the same. When I awoke, Planet Earth was still here. People were living their lives. I reminded myself, "It's just a dream." I found therapy for myself because I couldn't tell anyone. When I did confide in a couple of people, they laughed and said, "What are you smoking? You must be crazy." So, I decided not to tell anyone else. I used the phrase, "It's just a dream," to sustain my energy and exist like everyone else.

One night I wasn't flying. It was like I had no wings. I tried to lift, but there were no wings, so I had no power. It was like my wings were cut off. They were falling; I could not flap them. That night was the scariest of them all. I couldn't fly. So, I had to run along with everyone else who was running. Adults were running. The children were running, everyone. I looked up, trying to look for the older woman. She was nowhere to be found. I couldn't hear her voice. I had no idea where she was or if she had even been summoned.

As we ran, a giant snake came from the ground. His head was more extensive than his whole body, about a quarter kilometer wide. His mouth was bright white, like a light. The snake was sucking the earth, and the ground, eating and swallowing everything in its path. Then suddenly, my wings sprang up, and I started to fly. I saw a friend from school whom today became my son's mother in real life. We were not in love back then. I barely knew her. The snake was about to swallow her, and she called, "Parish, Parish, are you just going to leave me here?" Parish was my nickname.

I was scared. I don't like snakes in the dream or real world, and I certainly didn't want the snake to eat me. But I couldn't leave her. I went back for her. I picked her up by the shoulder with my foot. I didn't see it and didn't know if it was a foot or claw, but I just picked her up. And then a guy who was about to be eaten by the snake grabbed her leg, trying to pull her down, and started to take her with him. She pushed him away. I picked her up and took her to the sky, to the cloud; we both vanished into the cloud; I dropped her off somewhere and told her I would be back. I needed to help the children. I picked up as many children as possible and dropped them off at the same place. After everything calmed down, I didn't see her after that.

The war ended. Planet Earth was devastated again. The same night, I double-dipped. It was the same Planet, Earth, and the same war continued. And double dip, I cannot fly. We were still running. We were running on the edge of cliffs. Beneath the mountains was a lake with lots of fish. Big fish. You could catch them, put them on your plate, and go and eat. We spent a few nights there; other people were there, too, not just me. But then suddenly, I found myself alone, wandering in the forest.

A black woman showed up. She wore black silk covering like a fishnet all over her skin. She said, "Come with me. Let's go this way." The road is divided into two parts, one going north and the other south. She said, "Come with me. Let's take this road; it is not bumpy."

I replied, "Why don't you come with me? It's not bushy; it's low trees."

"No, she replied; there is nothing where you are going. I am not going with you if you go that way," she said.

I looked at her. She was lovely. She had a great butt, nice tits—big ones—and a skinny stomach. But I didn't want to go with her. For some reason and I felt something was wrong. She kept trying to convince me to follow her. I asked her if the older woman had sent her. She wondered who that was, and I told her she was the guardian.

"No, I don't know any guardian," she replied. "I am just here to help you."

"No, I cannot go with you. But you can come with me if you want." When she said no, I told her, "OK, I will go my own way, and you go yours."

I started to wander in the forest all by myself. Then I met a group of people. Lots of them. They suggested that I come with them. When I asked them where they were going, they didn't say. Their answer didn't seem necessary to me. I just kept going my way.

The same night I came to my father's mountains in my homeland. Then I remembered that I had been on that mountain in the real world. The best part of my dreams is that I know I am dreaming. There are six mountains around the village. All the villagers shared the hills. My father's village has its mountain; my mother does. And my brother-in-law's as well. I have access to three peaks, which I can freely soar around.

My father has told me that my ancestors lived at the far end of the mountains many years ago. There was no water or electricity there; you couldn't grow crops there either, so there was no need to go there; my father never took me there before he passed away. But they always told us the stories of the mountains, even though we weren't allowed to go there.

Well, one day I decided to take my friends to the mountains. It took between thirty and forty minutes to climb the hill. It's not a rock mountain but giant hills that stretch more than a thousand feet high. At the top, you can see everything. My father was correct; there was a fence around his house and an entrance made with stone and red mud. I went in first and saw a baby antelope standing there. My father later said it was a gift. One of my friends tried to pick it up. I pushed him away and picked it up myself.

When I got home, I told my mother all that had happened. She was happy but wondered why we decided to go there. When I told my father, he said, "That is the origin of our ancestors."

I tried to help the antelope survive. I didn't have enough money to buy milk, and it died four days later.

Before going to the mountains, I refused the sexy woman and the group. I ended up in my father's mountains. I knew exactly where I was; I had been there in the real world. I stood there as long as I could. Suddenly my wings just returned, then I flew. I didn't go to space, though there was no reason to go there; the war ended. Lots of humans have died, and there is not much left.

So I went home. This time I went to Africa. As always, I sat on the roof of my house in the village. I was still in the dream world. I watched my mom; she couldn't see me. Then I returned to Canada as always. It didn't take long to get from Africa to Canada. Two minutes max. When I returned to Canada, I woke up, took a shower, and got ready to go to work, just like everyone in the real world.

Another night was one of the most restless nights I have had. I was summoned. I usually know the faces of the people who demand of me. They are traditionally my ancestors, my father, and those great men who will become something in the future. But this night, no one was there. It was just me. I could see the sun so close to me. I could see bubbles on the surface of the sand, like when you are boiling something. But this time, it was not just boiling. It was twenty times stronger than boiling water. It's like boiling rice with no cover on the pot at the highest degree. It started spitting out flares. Again, I saw the sun sending solar flares all over space, traveling to the earth, and burning everything in its path, including the moon, this time. The earth's surface was burned to ashes and red soil. The seas and the oceans dried sixty percent. I saw humans living around the shorelines. Whatever was left of the waters was because of some deep part of the oceans, the mountains, and volcanoes dormant beneath the sea before the event took place. That was the only place you could find humans.

The solar flame cleaned up the earth's surface. But Planet Earth was still alive in some parts. There was no damage to her. She was still standing.

The blue world, the beauty of all beauty, the home of the stars. I like to think that is where I come from originally.

The war has ended. I didn't think it was going to end, but it ended. There have always been wars of different kinds. When it ended, my father came to my house. He wasn't alive in the real world but lived in a dream world. He didn't say anything to me then, but sometimes, I hear his thoughts and advice on what to do or say when I'm in a bad situation. And other times, we talked, but not in the palace when everyone was talking. This palace has no thrones or kings, like in the real world.

In the dream world, it is just an expanse of space in another world, another dimension called the Blue World, a place where I am free from this world. Blue World is everything for me; it is where my power reigns Supreme. For every dreamer in this world, the power of transcending comes from the dream world. The Blue World is known as Blue Planet. It is the most beautiful place I have ever dreamed of, a place for small gods like me can thrive. My father described it to me long ago, when I was a child. I didn't know what it meant until now. I will translate it from my language to English. The power of the Blue Planet was given to me by my father. It was my birthright. It belonged to me. And after I have lived my time here on earth, it will belong to my sons and their children before and after.

The freedom of flying was not the only gift with the blue planet; It also came with the ability to make good decisions without fear of failure. It was like a blank check, and one had to be aware of greedy relatives who would try to steal it. But sometimes, they succeeded in stealing it, but they didn't know how to harness that power. Then they forgot about it, and it would return to the owner. Most of the time, they fought without knowing who or what they were fighting for.

"Nevo" is my biological family's tribe name in Igboland, Enugu state Nigeria, and I think we are standing in the Centre with direct access to the Blue planet. where the dream world and the real world meet, the center of all things. The wall between the dream world and this world is very tin; that's why most people dream and communicate with people from the other side. I have flown there tons of times. I can have whatever I want in the dream world. I will manifest it in the real world if I choose to.

Do you remember when I told you, you could take what you want and throw away what you don't, or you could give it to them? When I said, "give it to them," I meant to give it to those who deserve it, those who hurt or envy you. A hypocrite is worse than a hater. A hater will have nothing to do with you, exchange clothes in the dressing room, or ask you for makeup if you're a girl. But a hypocrite and jealousy will eat with you at the same table, share your stories, and hear your darkest secrets, and you won't know that they are against you. So, I loved the hater more than the hypocrite or the jealous one. With the hater, you go your way, and I go mine. I do not hate the hypocrite or the jealous one; I dislike them. Their mindset is so cheap. Once they get caught, they will say, "I am just human. I make mistakes, and I am sorry." Like sorry, I will fix all the damage that person has done. Because you are a minor god, you forgive the person because you know who you are; they know you are more remarkable than they are, and everyone knows it; because of this; as long you are here on earth will always encounter people like this; don't be upset with them use their power for your benefits, by laughing when they hate you can feel the vibration of the energy you pull and transform from them and use it to nourish yourself; just like eating ice-cream in the hot sun.

When I say "small gods," what does that mean? When a daughter of God and son of God meet and join together in love and happiness, when they have a child automatically become a minor god, five times more potent than ordinally human, and they have access to both worlds to go as they please.

If you study it correctly, the secret the Blue World holds is that it brings fortune and prosperity to the real world. The wealth in real life, the people who will come into your have a job to help you even get weather. I cannot categorize all dreams as unreal or accurate; I am not saying I am interpreting them because I don't. I try not to mix up dreams with the real world. It's confusing sometimes. So, I will talk about Blue Planet later. Maybe in this book, maybe in the next. But let's continue with the dreams. We have spoken of the war. We have talked about the beauty of stars and everything else we have seen. Now let's talk about the machines.

Chapter 8

The Machines

The first machine I saw in the dream world was the one that stopped hurricanes. Let me take you to how it was built and how I saw it. The first time I saw it, I wanted to know how it was built and works. So, I opened the top of the engine. The core was made with fire, like burning fire, lava-like moving machines; sprockets and chains were in the main central Four steel bars in the four corners of the machine held each track. It looked like an excavator but a hundred times bigger. As they move, they stretch to almost twenty kilometers long.

On the seashore, they are connected. The machine has separation joints that come apart, allowing you to move it from one location to another. There is a blade, like a wall, on the side of the machine as it stretches to thirty kilometers long. A metal wall about five hundred millimeters thick on the side of the device that faces the ocean: behind the machine, on the side that faces land, is a steel bar going above the engine to the other track of the device. These also come apart, facilitating the machine's moving from location to location. They look somewhat like machines we use today in the oil fields in the real world.

That is all the information I have about these machines. As I said, the dream and natural worlds are a bit confusing. These fragments give you the idea if you ever want to build a machine to stop hurricanes.

Based on my calculations, fire in the bottom of the machine generates enough hot pressure to reach at least five hundred million pounds of force per square inch PSI, accumulating the power of a system deliberately designed for one purpose only. This is extremely powerful with a mixed combination of hot and cold air.

So, when the wave of a hurricane comes in front of the blade on the metal wall, multiple nozzles allow air to pass through. Some nozzles are diagonal, some are straight, and some are at an angle that allows the stand to rotate with that pressure. When the first wave from the hurricane comes, the pressure is released at least three kilometers before the storm reaches the shoreline. This drives all the water from the beach back to the sea by creating a wave and pushing it back toward it. The waves collide with the sea three kilometers between the machine and the shoreline. The water bounces back, and the engine automatically shuts down the pressure for a couple of minutes, allowing the water to flow slowly back to the shore. Then it will bounce back to the metal wall. The water will not be as high as before, but it will return. The pressure automatically restarts and pushes more waves toward the ocean or the sea and waits for the second hurricane wave, always worse. The machine does this over and over again.

I looked inside the main engine room after I opened the core. Inside are regulators. There is a computer screen attached to the wall. It is divided into quadrants with GPS locations. This tells the machine where the hurricane will be stronger and where it will hit next. This machine is designed to self-sustain itself electrically.

I flew around the machine and watched how it worked repeatedly. When it was built, the only objective was to focus on where there were only human inhabitants in cities. The most beautiful part of this machine is that people can continue their lives without worrying about hurricane preparation, like boarding up windows or climbing to the roof of a building and trees when a hurricane hits. Once the cyclone is detected and the wind reaches fifty kilometers an hour, the machine goes into operation, protecting the city from damage or destruction. The current flows upward, spreading over thirty thousand feet across the clouds until it dissipates while the city stays safe.

Let's talk about the night I saw a machine that stopped tornadoes. The same rules applied to this machine but with a different design. It operates under heavy pressure, the same as the hurricane machine. But because tornadoes are localized, they are easier to stop than hurricanes. All you need to do is break it in half or as much as possible. The machine has two large nozzles. Steel tanks are attached to the device. Each tank is about a hundred millimeters thick and can hold more than three hundred million pound-forces per square inch; PSI. They are empty, waiting for the tornado to touch down. When the tornado is about half a kilometer away, an air gunshot into the center of the tornado, with the vacuum facing the tornado's root. The air gun divides the tornado in half. A second shot shoots upward into the air. The bottom part is vacuumed into the tank and released toward the nozzle, spreading it all over the sky and allowing it to break further. The tornado vanishes into thin air, and the blue sky appears.

The tornado machine's control system is different. It's made with pressure and hot hydraulics. The interface can project the location of tornados when they detect signals for destruction.

When I saw these machines for the first time, I was amazed. All I could think of was how to build them here on Planet Earth. It would have been much more accessible if I knew how to draw. But I don't. This is the only way to explain how the machines work and what I saw. I hope someone will figure out how to build these machines one day, though I could make them myself if I had access to resources. I hope someone will be able to create them with the fragments I have offered and provide them with ideas. You can always look me up for information and answers about how to build it. I saw no manuals or measurements. What I provided is from my memory approximates.

Before we talk about space homes, I want to tell you that the first time I saw them in the dream world was on my way to Saturn. They're wonderful. I could not help but wonder how they could build a house in a space with no foundation. The houses are hung in space with no foundations, unlike those here. The homes have windows and rooms but are not attached to anything. They look like they're floating in the sky. The houses were beautifully coordinated with each other. I was excited to build the space home myself. The entire time I traveled to Saturn and saw the space homes, I was excited and amazed.

When I woke up, all I wanted to do was build a space home; imagine waking up in the morning feeling this way, the excitement, knowing that you just came from another world similar to earth, and seeing all this, there is no feeling like it. I was full of energy and eagerness. I could see how I could make it. And then, What if? Came to mind, as did How? My enthusiasm started to diminish, but I knew I might be ahead of my time. I wouldn't say I liked that feeling. I said, "You know what, there has to be a way to build this house." Then I applied the acronym STAR to this situation in my mind. In my daily life, work, exams, appointments, interviews, and so on, I use the STAR process to help me navigate situations, handle things, and achieve my goals. It always works if I am consistent without any deviations. STARS stands for *s*ituation, *t*ask, *a*ction, and *r*esult. And from the results, you know how you did.

Then I asked myself, "How will I get a house up in the sky?" I realized it was not sky but space. This meant the house must follow the earth's gravitational laws. Now how do we get a house up in the space? It hit me from the dreams. I thought about the tornado machine that shoots pressure in the sky. Can I shoot a house into space? I thought, wow, that will require much pressure. Imagine if that were possible. But how would we shoot home to the space? Unless the house is made of heat resistance materials, as an air balloon compresses into a rocket, including the people who will live in it and everything they need inside. Another idea: First, I need to build a stainless-steel house, steel that won't bend or break. We will then calculate the mass and use Einstein's $E=mc^2$ Quote. So, we have to figure out the weight of the house and how far it will travel to space with the pressure gun to shoot it up into space. It will require lots of pressure. All these are just hypotheses.

Then we have to worry about thin air. You will get to the tin air a hundred kilometers above sea level, which is hard to breathe. Building a house in space has to have a self-sustainable energy-recycling system for everything from cooking to showering. An oxygenated system purifies, recycles, and regenerates' fresh air as needed, flowing throughout the house and providing fresh air. The home must have an attached separate pressure source built from an air compressor system powered by solar energy that can push it from one place to the other. Another thing I think is possible is to figure out how to make rain in the air in space the same way we make rain here on earth with electric charges.

Another question is, how will people find food? Since the house will not be designed with agricultural systems. How can they survive? Should they have a farm in the place? Where would the food and water come from? Those are other challenges to my idea of building a space home.

Then I came up with the world's tallest mountains to build home space stations. I then realized there had to be a way to attach elevator shafts that pushed out like a telescope. These elevators would be attached to the elevators at the bottom of each house, so there is a place in the space grid based on how the homes are designed and the stop points in each mountain. The purpose of the elevator is to create a hollow point that stretches at least a hundred thousand feet; every hundred thousand feet, there's drones a platform for recharging. This elevator is made of thin aluminum material, allowing air through and restoring more air for circulation in the homes.

Another purpose of this elevator is to allow drones to pick up food and water from mountain stations for distribution to space homes. That is the only way for the people who live there to survive. It is the same way a person can travel to earth in a pod. Another way a person can travel from a space home to Earth is via a drone that is big enough to gravitate slowly before releasing a parachute, thereby saving battery power to five hundred to one hundred feet before releasing the drone's energy source, which provides enough ability to land without consuming too much energy. That's another option to travel from space home to earth.

The elevator usually floats up to the space home. The elevator is attached to the house only when it is shot up to space. Remember, this is just hypothetical.

Aza is a mountain in my dreams. The peak of my father's mountain. That is where I saw the disk for the first time. It's a machine. The top of this machine is made of thick, deep-blue, metallic glass. I can feel the thickness by looking at it. All those deep blues are made of solar panels that create solar energy to power the disk for millions of miles and can travel further in space. The higher it flies toward the sun, the more the temperature rises, which heats those solar layers. That forces it to generate more solar energy than it needs because of the excessive energy the electric current surge circulates, which creates a core point that makes the disk fly ten times faster.

There is always enough energy for a time to come. The battery won't be working by then. The battery's job is to run the main electric motor, which can generate enough power for five twenty-story buildings. In that power comes the source of all power. And then, that will create the final process of sustainable energy. Once you have that, you have to create a platform made of thick stainless steel and raw galvanized plates, three to four millimeters in thickness.

There are six of them; attach them. Then you create exhaust ports made with the finest galvanized material. A two to three-foot exhaust pipe will have access to the manifold of the center pressure. There will be at least thirty holes in those plates I created. These exhaust pipes will go through the holes around the disk. And there will be a six-inch stainless steel plate from the bottom of the disk to the top.

After that, I need to create steel sticks similar to cylinders used in car power-steering systems and Spicer bearings. Instead of four angles, there will be eight. Every exhaust has two rings to connect to the power steering systems. All the parts are made with the finest quality of all elements needed.

The disk is made of two parts: the bottom and the top. I saw the compressor's tiny ones with small pumps attached to the head installed on the plates. These have holes with exhaust pipes and small tanks connected directly to the lines. The tank's electronic regulator controls the pressure, and at the end of the tank are hydraulic pipes connecting all the tanks. This pushes the air when it is most needed, especially when navigating.

The solar panels are tiny but strong and almost weightless. Each bundle comprises six solar panels stacked together, and each cell is attached to the other. The solar panel itself is about six feet high and three feet wide. It is about 90 degrees in circumference.

The base of the disk is about fifty feet by fifty feet in circumference. The top is forty-five feet by thirty feet in circumference. The six stacked solar panels act as a roof for the top part of the disk. Additional bundles of solar panels will go around the bottom part. The top and bottom pieces only differ in their rotation in different directions. The bottom part rotates clockwise; the top part rotates counterclockwise.

The first and second parts of the bottom base have a fan ring that rolls around it and is attached to the outside of the disk. The purpose of these electric motors is to recycle air that floats to the cab on the bridge's interior. The hoses that will pass through these fans are made of breathable material. Every cab, both the bottom and top, is pressurized, just like an airplane. This means it will be completely welded and sealed with pressure control, inspected, and holiday tested.

These are the parts we need to build this disk. But before the skeleton of the disk is constructed, we must ensure that every hole, angle, hook, or port is constructed and installed. This disk won't be running on the ground, looking for an airport to fly in and out of. It can land anywhere based on size. And it won't need a blade, like a helicopter. It will have an edge on the top but for navigation purposes. It won't be able to lift off the ground like a helicopter. It will lift on its own anywhere, anytime. On the bottom, there will be a jet engine. I don't build jet engines; it is only how I saw it. The jet engine will be used with chemical fuel, though fusion-derived energy is better because the machine is tiny, and there is not enough room to carry fuel. The purpose of fission fuel, U-235, will be the best recommended for the disc to help it travel faster to orbit before it burns out. The engine doesn't need much fission fuel as I am not traveling to different planets. It simply helps the disk to lift off the ground. If it is flying at the same speed in the sky within the earth's atmosphere, we need to fill the tank with fission fuel now and then, depending on where we are going.

There is so much I can tell you about the computer system. But for now, I will tell you what it consists of: communication equipment, self-sustainable energy, a self-controlled system (like autopilot), and a security system. The security system includes mini-drones with cameras that check for damages on the solar panels outside the disk. They follow the disk-like flies following buffalo. They will notify the interface on the main bridge if there is any damage to the solar panels or any system. They will inform the bridge about issues regarding security threats, damage control, and asteroids within a two-kilometer radius.

As for the navigation system, most of the controls are touchscreens and manual buttons. If I lose control, I can manually and safely land the disk. That is why the disk was built in the bottom and top parts. The top part is the control center, where you control the disk; the base is mostly for compressors and other features that make the engine disk work, including the jet engine and fission fuel tank. It was built that way, so if there were a fire on the fission fuel tank or any leak that would cause fires, the disk's top and bottom parts could be separated. The top part has no engine, only parachutes to land safely on the ground. That is the safety system we are talking about right now. Let's say, for example, that the cab or bridge catches fire. It is the same system and control. The only difference is a small compartment in the bottom part of the cab that can only hold one person. A computer there will help the bottom portion to navigate without parachutes up to eight thousand feet. Then the parachute will be released and help you land gently on the ground.

But there is still a risk. The fusion fuel and jet engines are made of cramped keys. Fusion fuel is hazardous and requires tremendous energy; it can create faster acceleration than regular fuel, and the jet engine has flames on it. They are right there in front of you. To release the cramps in the interface of the computer system, fusion fuel on the one hand and jet engine on the other. You pull upward. The cramps cannot be released if there is a fire or emergency because if you remove them, they won't reattach.

There are other safety features. The control system compartments for the bottom part of the disk are made of silicone and insulation, the softest microfiber. The person doesn't suffocate because the fresh air system stops working. The only air that will be there is previous air that has been compressed.

We need to calibrate the pressure to lift that much weight into the sky. For example, if we have three kilograms, we need at least twenty-seven kilograms of air pressure to lift it from the ground: 3^9 = 27 kilograms. So you have to ensure that the electric motors and the tanks on the base of the disk can generate that much pressure. Suppose you want to stay in the earth's atmosphere. But in space, it can use the earth's gravitational pull and won't need that much pressure, just a bit to navigate. You will need it when you get back to the earth's atmosphere.

The disk does not run entirely on a combustion engine. It runs on a combustion and pressure engine. Together, they create a sustainable and warming environment, serving to heat the cab, which will be cold. We will have an air-conditioning system as well. As I mentioned earlier, the closer you get to the sun, the more energy the solar cell will produce, which will heat the roof and the cab, and we will need a cooling system more like a sauna, where hydrogen is mixed with water and forms water vapor. The water vapor will help recycle all the waste from the sewage system. The recycling machine will comprise a traditional recycling system—mud, ocean sand, gravel, dry leaves, earth, and minerals—compartment by compartment.

I need to know how much water I can recycle in a minute, ten minutes, an hour, or a day in the recycling system. And how much water is vaporized through the recycling time? For example, you do not get ten cups if you recycle ten cups. Instead, you get eight or eight and a half cups. During the recycling process, hundreds of milliliters of water are lost. So, it's essential we know how much water we have and that there is a computer system that recycles everything automatically.

Water and air are the most important elements the human body needs. Next are food and sleep. So, we ensure these needs are met accordingly, including overriding manual settings.

Now it is time to build the disk. I will measure everything, including the disk's skeleton's diagonal, horizontal, exterior, and interior. You can find the measurement specifications earlier in this chapter. We need to build a structure that consists of three flat stainless-steel bars. Three more will be made with thick-profile aluminum with hangers, bottom base units, a four-inch maintenance hole, and assorted holes for data and electrical wires and plumbing holes. Measurements must be accurate for every system. Everything will be made using the finest quality elements I mentioned previously. That is how I saw it in the Blue World on my way to Saturn.

If you want to build this machine, you have to figure it out. The information I have provided is the most crucial part. Follow these instructions. Everything else will be easy for you to comprehend.

Chapter 9

The Choices

I was there. I had just landed. I was coming from Mars. As mentioned in the first chapters, I carried Planet Earth in my hands. I opened it and squeezed inside. I came home to Planet Earth. Suddenly I found myself sitting with my father and grandfather. Other people were there, but I cannot remember their faces now. They asked me, "What do you want?"

I replied, "What is going to happen? Is there a price if I want something?" They didn't say anything. My father just looked at me. They brought me a snake and an alligator and asked me to choose one. I said, "I want them both."

They told me, "You cannot have both. You must choose one."

"No, I want both of them."

"If you want both of them, capture them both."

I thought it would be easier to capture the alligator. I can track the snake's slither through the sand. I will be able to know where it is and can catch it. So, after I captured the alligator, I followed the snake to a black cave. I went inside a little bit until the sunlight started to fade. And I told myself, "If I continue with no sunlight, I will die." So, I flew out of the cave, picked up the alligator I had captured with my foot, and took it away. That was my first choice.

One thing about choices is that it's like a decision. If the choice has already been made, then the decision has no value. No matter what you decide, the choice has already been made. So, how can it be a choice if the decision has already been made? If the decision has already been made, then the option has no value either, which brings us to the highest note of the low is the lowest note of the high. You can't have one without the other.

The second choice was when I was searching for something in Blue World. I was looking for a blue crystal stone. It was not just a blue crystal; it was more like a metallic stone mixed with blue. I never found it. I just stopped looking for it.

I carried Planet Earth in my hands, like always. I opened the cloud, and through it, I flew straight to my village in my homeland. Then my father summoned me; my uncle was called as well. My uncle said he should be sitting on the throne, but my father said, "No, it is not your birthright. It is my son's, even though he is young. He can appoint anyone he wants to sit on the throne until he comes of age." My uncle was furious but had no choice since my father had decided.

Then my father presented two items. One was a gold pendant that looked like an E, but there was no center bar like an E. The second item was a plant that grows in the mountains where I come from. The only place to find that plant is on the high tops of the mountains, where it grows two feet tall. The plant can live for more than twenty years. It grew more on the ground than on the surface. Even when a forest fire burns half the species away, it will rise to two feet tall in three to six weeks.

The second choice was to pick between the gold and the plant. When my father presented it, my uncle rushed and grabbed the gold. It was like my father knew he was going for the gold pendant. I looked at my father to see what he was going to do. Was he going to yell at or beat up my uncle? My father smiled. He picked up the plant and gave it to me. He told me, "Leave the gold for him. This one is better. I never quite understood how plant is better than gold until later days in my life. I knew that something could be broken entirely and could still be fixed. Never give up tomorrow is always brighter than today.

Showering with gold occurred during Christmastime on earth. I was flying. I wasn't going anywhere specific. I was just having fun, releasing my wings and flying in every direction. Then I was flying deep in the mountains. They were not like the mountains I knew. They had eyes. Their peaks were so sharp, unlike my homeland's smooth mountains.

I was flying low. It was cold, but the cold didn't bother me. What bothered me was that I didn't plan my navigation. I was flying too low, and the mountain was so high. I couldn't have flown above it if I had tried. So, I sprinted toward the mountain, jumped on it, sprung myself five kilometers back to where I was coming from, built-up momentum, and when I got close to the mountain's peak, I flew above it.

Then I started to descend into a playing field with many people there. It was like a market. Everybody was going in different directions. Everyone knew where they had to go, including me, a lake with fogs separating the mountain and the plane field fifty feet deep around the mountains. You have to swim in the water and climb the mountains to get to the other side; no one knows what is on the other side; all I know is that I have to get there. It doesn't matter if it's better or worse, but something good is happening on the other side, with everyone heading in the same direction. The feeling is that I will see God. Some people found it easy to get to the top. Some people walked there like there was a bridge above me like it was nothing. And I had to swim to the mountain base; it is like everyone has their tracks; guess what my track is? And erosion. It was so hard to swim already. When I started to climb, the mountain was falling backward toward me. I couldn't use my wings; it was so high. I struggled. I spent months climbing that mountain. I spent weeks in some places. One good thing about the dream world is that you don't get hungry; food and hunger don't exist.

And one day, I finally climbed to the top. I opened my eyes to see what was on the other side, but I couldn't get them open. I tried to force my eyes to open to see what was going on, but my eyes were stuck close. Then suddenly, I saw myself drop six feet—a setback. But I made it through again. I found myself walking on the street, and I saw the stars. People threw gold at me. A bucket filled with gold was filled, and they poured it over me. It was dripping as I walked.

Then I saw the city of men. It was a beautiful city. But I felt different energy there. I'm still not sure what kind of energy it is. But I was like a king there, but something was missing; I ruled as king over this place for as long as I could remember until I woke up.

Inspiration versus manipulation is not from the dream world. At least, that is my conclusion based on my opinion analysis of the dream world. When I awoke from flying dreams, this was my life in the real world. The calculation between the real and dream worlds can never be correct, even though the intersection is precise in recurring dreams. Something is always different because everything seems real in the real world. But in the dream world, it's the same reality. It's just that the dream world has no rules as the real world does. The real world is the most dangerous place to exist as a human being. As I take the human form, it is tough to exist because you have to live as everyone else does in the human world here on earth. You must work, take your children to school, make money, and pay your bills. If you get married, you must take care of your spouse and maybe have a beer and hang out with friends. This is what human beings do; if you do this, you will blend in.

Spending time with humans, you will see the best of them. Humans are adorably beautiful, especially my children; I am exhausted by their love and laughing, how they love each other, how they build their cities, and how they help each other in time of need; even though some of them have left their post as human guidance and still care if their neighbor has problems, and the women are gorgeous. They caught my eyes now and then, even though I was not part of them. I am not like them. I respected and adored this species, and yet I am human.

The dream world is boundless, where anyone can be anything, good or bad. But nothing compares with manipulating one human against another in the real world. People often seem reasonable at first with bad intentions. This is a problem with humans. It's like a disease of the mind, incurable, like greediness. So you understand me; I am not judging anyone. No one is allowed to judge others. But we must talk about it to know and resolve it because what seems wrong to you might seem right to someone else. It's a difference in mindsets. Others simply come to help and inspire you, to believe that a person can be worth more than a million dollars. We are all heroes within ourselves; anyone can be anything. Some figure out how to get over the mind's bridge that connects soul and body. Others need a little push. You would be surprised at how much people can accomplish with a bit of inspiration. Believing in someone is the most critical type of esteem you can offer someone. Please keep up the excellent work; remember that what you give, you shall receive.

It was an ordinary night. I wasn't flying in space. Instead, I was flying low between the sky and earth. That was the first time I saw the older woman since the war. She wasn't in the space as usual. I saw her while I was flying low to the ground. I landed and folded my wings. We were walking on this narrow road, and she asked me how I was doing. I told her everything was good. Then she told me she had something to show me.

She took me to the belly of the smooth mountain. There a man covered with white chalk was floating in the sky. I could see his eyes; they were tiny and slanted. He asked me, "What do you want in life?"

I asked him, "What is going to happen?" My answer should have been, "My heart's desire," because that was exactly what I wanted in life. This is probably the third time I have been asked what I want.

He looked at me with disappointment and asked me again, "What do you want?"

I replied, "Can you give me 6/49 lottery numbers?"

He said, "OK," as he brought out his journal and wrote it down.

The older woman told him, "Do not give it to him."

I asked her, "Why can't I have the numbers?"

He shrugged. He looked at me and then at the old lady. "You heard her. She is your guardian, so I will listen to what she says."

That was the first time I realized she was my guardian. I looked back at the man, and he looked back at me slyly, which could only mean one thing: "I love you like my son, but I cannot give you the gift you ask of me. You are too young for it." I looked at the older woman again, and she was smiling. I was angry with her for not letting me have the lottery numbers. I left her and walked further down the road, where cashew and mango trees were overbearing with ripe fruit. This was the perfect season to pick them from the ground. I ate both and then stretched my wings and flew to the sky.

With that anger, I had no direction or planned to go anywhere. I just kept flying. I reached the center of the universe in space. I stood there for a long time. I walked in an area as I walked on the street in the real world. I looked around at the four corners of the universe. There was nothing there. Nothing at all. Just space. Then I dived back home at full speed, racing with my wings at 60 degrees instead of 90 degrees. I passed stars, planets, and the moon and landed in Toronto, Canada.

That night taught me that manipulation might benefit you, even though you disagree. But the only people you can believe in their manipulations are your parents or guardians. They will never lie to you; everything they do is for your benefit. It might seem hard and misunderstand at the time, but sooner or later, you will realize it was the best for you.

One thing I haven't explained much about is how I feel when I wake up. Or how the dream world affects my daily life. As I said initially, I separate the natural world from the dream world. Some of the dreams come true, maybe only 20 percent. Sometimes the plans are not only about you or related to you. It could be about someone you met in the middle of the day at a restaurant, an office, or even school. When something starts happening to the person, good or bad, and you are present, you may begin to understand that you have seen this situation before. You will recall you have seen it in the dream world. Most times, perhaps about 30 percent, you could be right and predict how that incident ends. Knowing how it ends positively affects your mind, for example, when it involves a marriage proposal, promotion at work, or a dispute between two people. You already know how this will end because you have seen it before. Sometimes I am excited to tell them how it ends, but I withdraw because I am not allowed to interfere. Even if it's terrible news, I am not allowed to interfere. However, if it is a circumstance in which someone could get hurt, I must intervene. If they oppose me, I have no choice but to tell them how it ends. And in those circumstances, I am usually correct.

Except for the situations I mentioned earlier, manipulation is very insulting and disrespectful behavior, especially to friendship or relationships, whatever the relationship is. It could be with your boss, partner, or the delivery guy who brings pizza to some rich dude living in a penthouse. That is how insulting manipulation could be. Again, I am not judging anyone, but I must explain this. Jealousy, love, hate, and hypocrisy are the roots of manipulation. I would rather have a friend who hates me than a friend who is envious of me. A friend who hates me will not have a business partnership with me and will not invite me to his wedding or his daughter's birthday party. But a friend who is envious of you will eat at the same table and still be jealous of you. Jealousy and envy are the same, except envy have a good side. Yes, you can envy someone in a good way. For example, if you have struggled in life and see someone who has been where you are and made it, you can cheer that person on. You want to be like them, so you envy them in a good way. But jealousy doesn't have a good side; no matter what you do for this person, you can give the individual the heavens and earth, and still, it would never be enough.

On the other hand, inspiration is everything. Every human being deserves to be inspired at least once. It's more effective in teens. That way, they can be encouraged throughout their lifetimes. When I was in my teens, a man used to come to my uncle's paint shop. He would always ask me, "Why are you here? You can do much more than just being here and selling paint."

I used to have soccer class and training after school and still go to a paint shop to help as little as possible when the paint shop was closed and still do my chores. When he said that, I thought, I am doing more than selling paint. I am also playing soccer. This soccer training was complimentary and provided by the community. Every village has its community in the city; because of this, they hold tournaments every Christmas and New Year. If twenty people from one village lived in a town, they came together every Sunday to ensure everyone was in good health. They contributed fifty nairas to the community purse for emergency reasons. They created a children's soccer team made up of friends and family. When Christmas came, we went to the village where we played against different teams from different states in Nigeria.

Chapter 10

It's Like a Day without Rain

A day without rain is when everything is exactly how you want it to be. Every human has that blessed day. When you laughed so hard, your belly hurt. It's a great day, a day to remember. But it's not just one day. It comes from time to time. You will have that perfect day that makes life all worth it.

In the dream world, I have always known my enemies. Don't get me wrong; they are not humans. They are electric power lines and mountains, oceans, and trees. I have my challenges when landing from flying dreams. Looking for a perfect place to land is a big problem for me. I cannot just land anywhere; I need open space.

Some days are just perfect in the real world too. Just like a day without rain, I can see it. It's like the day my first son was born. I watched him grow in his mom's belly, slowly and slowly. And when he was born, he was just like me but more petite and beautiful. He changed my life. It was one of those perfect days, like when my second son was born. I had a two-year-old running around and a baby who didn't know how to move but wanted to run around like his brother. Each day I call a day without rain a beautiful day.

A day with rain was like when my mother suggested, "Let us go to the farm and plant maize, cassava, and yellow yam, like potatoes.

It is ready to harvest in three weeks." Those days I call a day with rain, the nurturing, waiting, checking the garden from time to time until crops are ready to be harvested. Rain brings food. It brings life in abundance. Another day without rain was when I won a big project as a contractor. That brought money, and money brought food to share as much as I could in my village. When you succeed, don't forget to give a helping hand to those in need, always show gratitude and thanks by making a little miracle for those in need, and remember you came to this world alone and will leave it alone. The only thing that will matter in the end is your deeds and how you live your life.

Every person has a purpose. Every person's purpose is hidden, and you must find it yourself. If you see something you think is your purpose, you should stick with it. My purpose is to help the poor in any way I possibly can. Helping someone else is the hardest thing a person can do, if not foolish. But I will always do my best to help the less fortunate because who knows how your life will turn out tomorrow. So, always be thankful.

Poverty is a disease that kills more people than HIV or COVID-19. And yet many people don't understand the impact poverty has in our world today. Every child, woman, and man on this earth has experienced suffering at some point. While others suffer and die because of poverty. No one cares or pays attention to the data from World Aid. Who makes sure that help goes to the people who need it the most, so it seems, but there are always people who are left behind, and that is where I come in.?

Most of the time, the United States or some charitable organization sends aid to other countries, like Iraq, North Korea, Sudan, Somalia, Eritrea, and Ukraine. But there is no guarantee that the money will go to those who may need it the most. The leaders of such organizations need paper trails to see where these funds go and how they are utilized. For example, building schools and women's shelters in a country or town where law enforcement has little to do; or is not even recognized as much is worse than the help itself; it is like snatching food out someone's mouth; that is how assistance promised and paid for someone that never arrived feels like.

And to make matters worse, the orphanages are abandoned buildings. And you know what happens to abandoned buildings; no one cleans or maintains them. So, I have come up with an idea for converting a former orphanage into an official school and redesigning it into a living elementary school. Not an orphanage. Children often go to school from different locations, which is a great thing to do for these children. But my idea is different. I want to create a revolutionary recreational center for the kids; as I mentioned earlier, sometimes the best gift you can give a child is a happy environment and a change of mindset, freeing that mind from being an orphan to a higher upgrade with respect. Because those children need attention more than those, who have their parents. The orphans are very smart; they know how to survive difficult times. They have been through a lot, and it is tough for them to trust anyone. But giving them an office school with cutting-edge technology will make them the best in the world. Do you know how I know? I am not an orphan, but I have lived like one, which is how I know. We need to change the orphanage to a school home. We can train and educate these children in school and give them the best life can offer. Considering this cutting-edge technology and what they have been through, you will know what I am saying is true.

There is another way I can explain to you what a day with rain means in a straightforward phrase. When a person asks you back in Africa, do you know what happens when the sun sets by the waterside? The answer is simple, a day without rain; it's like "standard timest" from the flying dream world. It means you will get precisely what you want, what you expect to have. But you have to wait. It will come when all is in your favor; you will see the heavens and earth freeze for you to pass. Every human has a center point; all they have to do is wait for it, imagine it, think about it often, and deviate all their thoughts towards it. I am not saying to stop living or going to work or paying your bills. I am saying that every human has a central point to skip time and transcend to a new state of life. To skip years in the future and jump to a higher purpose and meaningful life. If your time comes, this is how it happens. For six months to a year, your life will change automatically. It's called "heaven's bonus" as a living being. Everyone receives it. Whether you are bad or good, we all accept it differently. Even a terrible person will receive it. This gives that individual an opportunity to be a better person. If they continue the old ways, that is the individual's choice. But the ultimate gift is when one puts others first before him or herself.

Maybe that is what they choose to do in life, or perhaps it is what life throws to that person that makes him recognize the suffering of others. Maybe the individual is just some idiot who wastes all resources on others that may be laughing behind their back. Who knows? The only way to beat ignorance is to know. Comes to what I said earlier; help goes to those who need it the most.

Heaven's bonus is the best and the final state of mind and gift you will receive from God. And once given, it will remain with you.

I will give you everything you have asked of me on that day. You have nothing to ask because I have given you everything you have asked of me.

This is heaven's bonus. I am not making it up; I received it. I have also seen people who have received it. The question is, how would you know when you have received the gift? If the gift is within you, you should know it's time to skip to a new dimension within the real world. I will give you pieces of my experience in the real world. Always remember to separate the natural world from the dream world. They sometimes appear to be the same but are different planes of reality. When your heavenly bonus is around the corner, you will likely notice some setbacks in your life. Don't be afraid or alarmed. The universe is just clearing the way for new things. You will see most of your friends and even some family members and coworkers start writing you off; if your companion is not allowed to follow you to your new life, they are gone too; it will hurt, but later on, you will see the reason, they are not part of your new life. Keep your eyes open. It's coming; it's happening. And once it arrives, you will know. And then next time, if you notice all these changes, you already know what comes. Everyone else will be surprised. Some may even ask you. "Do you see things happening to you?" Some people will even ask how you can be so happy while all this happens. Your reply will be, "Faith, baby, faith with a deep smile."

Chapter 11

Diamond Flying Dream

One spring night, I went to bed during the pandemic but couldn't sleep. It was a rough night. I was not sad, I was not angry, and I was not super-happy. I went into the living room and sat on the couch. I put the TV on. Then I started falling asleep. I muted the TV, and after a few seconds, I passed out on the couch.

I first saw myself home in the mountains in Africa covered with diamonds. Like everywhere made of diamonds, it was bright and beautiful, more like Christmas lights but brighter. There were different shapes of stones. The blue crystal stone I searched for throughout the universe was waiting for me. I had traveled through time and space searching for that stone only to find it sitting at home. I started flying low to take a good look, to see clearly. I don't know if my eyes were deceiving me. No, they were not deceiving me. The majestic crystal stone had been there all along. I thought, Leave everything here. Now that I know where it is, I will come for it when I need it.

I flew away. This time I was not in space; I was here on earth. Do you remember when I told you that you have the right to take what you want and throw away what you don't wish? or give it to those who hate you? It takes energy to agree with yourself and do things like that to your enemies even when they don't want to see you succeed. If you don't like it, please try to reconsider not giving it to them. You know it's dangerous, and it will destroy them. It usually comes with words. The words you speak are compelling. Even during creation, God created almost everything with words. So be careful of the words you speak. Choose every word carefully.

If you want to give it to them, make sure your decision is accurately based on what they have done to you. It is not what has been done to you or what they did that matters. How it makes you feel will determine your punishment for them. But four consequences come with the package. Please take what you want, throw away what you don't want, or give it to them. Those are the three of them. The fourth one is when you are wrong. When you are wrong, everything you wish for that person you give it to, good or bad, will multiply seven times for you; you will suffer more than what you wanted. So be careful if you're going to carry on with this practice. Make sure they are undoubtedly wrong.

In my case, I will say farewell to those who write me off. Besides, I found my crystal stone. And to top it off, I found a city of diamonds that belongs to me. All is well.

That night I met my uncle. I could call him uncle, but he was too young to be called uncle. So I called him cousin. We traveled somewhere in the desert. There was an old mother. I knew her. She had a daughter, who was also there. Then suddenly, we all ended up in a cave with zero gravity. Diamonds are floating everywhere. We jumped into the cave and started to grab the diamonds. When my cousin showed me his diamond, my eyes went wide. I will not tell you what I saw next.

I started to fly up into the sky with the diamonds I had grabbed. I remember my mountain full of diamonds in the back of my head; I sighed with deep happiness, full of hope for the future. However, I continued flying across a big city. Oh, my God, it was one of the largest cities I had ever passed over. It took me four days to fly across the city. There were obstacles, like power lines, trees, high-rise buildings, and mountains. It was exhausting to get out.

When I finally got out, I stepped down on a bridge. Then I saw my cousin again. He was angry. I asked him what had happened, and he told me he had lost some of his diamonds. I gave him some of mine, and he smiled and left. I just flew away. It took me another two days to get out. Then I got out of the sky and lifted my wings. I still had the diamonds with me.

Then I awoke in the real world. I drank water and watched some TV. Then after about an hour, I passed out again. I started flying higher and higher. I could see all country and city maps from the earth. I was flying and watching and counting the cities' designs. I flew slowly and gently, flapping my wings but not too hard. It was amazing to fly through clouds and play around them. It was one of the best flying dreams I ever had.

Among the large mountains in my homeland, there is a small mountain we call a baby mountain. It's easy to climb to the top, and we always do so. On the left side of the mountain, there are the *ukwaka* and *nzu* stone types. You can eat these stones as they are very soft and tasty. They are significant sources of iron in our diets. Mainly suitable for pregnant women; everyone eats but is more familiar with pregnant women to help the baby grow strong and healthy. I was told that it also makes the skin stronger to withstand the sun.

Enough of talking about my homeland and culture. Let's continue my understanding of flying dreams and the Blue World, the city of stars, above all the gates of the heavens. What is my experience? After my research, it is clear that I categorized the times of dream occurrences and all analyses, including all the information from the Blue World and flying dreams. One thing is accurate: I cannot fly in the real world.

I am not here to discuss whether the world is ending or not, it is not my place to tell panic stories, but these messages need to be delivered to everyone.

Do you think humans were created from the big bang? I don't think anyone knows what's going on. The planet was built like a child's drawing. Do you remember when God created heaven and earth, Jesus was there? He was the Word of God. Everything that was created was made through him. So he must have been a child at the time of creation. Because he was the light, he was born with light. He was there from the beginning when God commanded the creation of heaven and earth. My point is that I do not know the truth about life. But look at the surroundings and the splendor that accompanies the sunrise every day, and you can see the beauty of creation on earth, like the trees, the animals, the butterflies, dogs, and cats. And mosquitoes. Please don't get me started on mosquitoes here in Canada. Mosquitoes ruin my summers.

Anyway, let's talk a little about our knowledge of creation. Everything God created, he made in pairs. I don't know if I have mentioned this before, but I am repeating it to ensure I give out all the information in pairs in the natural and dream worlds. They all have pairs. Here you have man and woman, water and fire, heaven and earth, significant and weak, land and sea, moon and sun. God even created a pair for himself, one of the angels called Satan. He's the bad guy, even though that was not what he was supposed to be. That angel had opinions the Father didn't endorse because they threatened creation itself.

In each pair, one is always greater than the other. Fire is more incredible than water, God is greater than Satan, man is physically more robust than a woman, and the sun shines brighter than the moon. And to top it off, the moon cannot shine unless the sun's light reflects on her. And she shines brighter and gives birth to stars. And the stars become the reflections of the universe; I watched the stars from the mountain in my homeland long ago when I was in my teens. Sometimes, I try to reminisce about those feelings as a child, but those are gone through the wind, and the rest bind to my thoughts. And I know I am part of them from the beginning. I am with them now, and they are with me.

This is where knowledge was born for all creation, from the father himself. God Almighty is known as Eze Chikuwa. The beginning and the end. First and last. Alpha and Omega. The Father of light. He created everything that was made.

We humans and everything else alive on earth, and the dead, we thank you for this life and life to come. My message is clear: It's about dreams. Dreams are not like imagination or daydreams or the things you wish for yourself when thinking.

Sometimes I travel into the future and see myself where I will be in twenty years. We are building Sun City, which will represent Biafra. If Nigeria and Biafra stay together, the city will represent Nigeria in twenty years. I am not here for partiality, and I am not here to be recognized by humans. I am here to give the gift of knowledge to those who intend to pursue it. So, Nigeria and Biafra neither matter. I will be glad for Biafra to be independent and gain her republic. And 60 to 65 million people is an excellent number to govern. That way, I can build Sun City successfully. Sun City is an eight-year project and will be an extraordinary establishment for the country. The objective is to attract investors, but we need to create our African industrial revolution; until that happens, no one will hear us. Building factories and industries are the city's sole purpose. It will be an icon for Nigeria or Biafra; it doesn't matter who is in charge to me. If Biafra has gotten its republic, great. If it is still with Nigeria, that's great too. All I need is full government support and financing. We have to invest our money somewhere everyone will benefit from. Enough is enough. I am Biafran. I am saying that I care about humanity, which is essential to me. And I hope. Humans will benefit from my knowledge and message from the real world and the flying dream.

Sun City is my ultimate goal in my dreams and the finality of my thoughts. When I finish building Sun City, I will be content even if it's the last thing I do. my hope and challenges will when Nigeria or Biafra recognizes each other and start thinking smarter than the rest of the world. That's where I will honestly believe our time has come, where everyone does their jobs so I can do my work. But if they haven't recognized each other, Biafra will have no choice but to go on its own and have its republic. If Nigeria refuses, they give Biafra no choice but to go its way anyway. Unless they decide to listen to Biafrans and their ideas, we can build infrastructure and businesses and work with world trade organizations that will allow us to manufacture and export our products, giving the government tax income. Yet they can't see the big picture, blinded by old hatred's relic mind, which has deprived every one the opportunities that foreign investors would have to bring to the table. Allowing investors to come in and invest requires constant energy. We will build a nuclear plant for electricity. That is a start.

Let's build the city, Sun City. First, we need to create four quadrants of a pentagon. At every intersection, we have sewage underground, connecting everywhere in the city. The city will be designed with a stable population, but there will be a 17.5 percent increase from the outside world every ten years. Foreign workers will be allowed a free visa to enter. These will range from construction laborers to doctors, lawyers, scientists, dancers, and artists worldwide. Here we will build the new Nigeria or Biafra, whichever comes first. Either way, I have to share my knowledge, thoughts, and imagination of great things to make them better for humanity.

I used to say, "Give me Nigeria; in two years, Nigeria will be like Canada." That is the minimum I can go because I must fix everything. Imagine if I set everything and built new worlds and new cities. There would be an excellent economy. I can make it self-sustaining energy, and it will be powerful enough to power hospitals, homes, hotels, and airports, depending on how much energy you want. We can then take down the power lines that disrupt my flying in the dream world. Trees can stay.

This will be my gift to Nigeria or Biafra and boost the economy. Within those two years, all the minerals and federal tax income oil revenue I have to separate crude oil revenue from other minerals, so my people know which is which, will be combined to clean up both the environment (government and private sectors), environmental control, infrastructure improvements and construction, and agricultural enhancements. Cultural and native laws will be recognized. This is the fundamental basis of building Sun City. You must have this information. Once you have the foundation, which is the sewage and connected to the river that is about thirty kilometers away, the city will be sitting on top of that area, and we will build dams. When we have all this ready, then Sun City has evolved. And then homes will be built. They will be mushroom-shaped skyscrapers. There will be a minimum of eight elevators with steel shafts. Metal bridges will connect the buildings. This will be in the Centre of my homeland, the home of the gods. Every human being is a small god since we are made in the image of God.

Chapter 12

If I were The President of Nigeria

I know what Nigeria needs. I am Biafran, which means I am only supposed to support Biafrans. But as I traveled around the world, I learned a few things about life. The northern Nigerians have minimum mineral resources compared to the east and south. And that is a massive problem in Nigeria. Most people in the north are farmers and are very good at it. By looking at Nigeria's problem, you will see that Nigeria has set itself for success at the outset, and the easterner is entrepreneurs; we see it in the growing Nigerian economy. Most of the minerals are located in Biafra land, so there will be consequences if you take Biafra away from them. Nigeria will fall. Even if it survives, it will be like a dead man walking. The northerners will no longer have direct access to Nigeria's energy policymaking, and that will unveil northern privilege on energy, sending them back to the time of independence; as a consequence of breaking Nigeria, desolation and poverty will rampage the people who will eventually be the end of Nigeria, while in the east even though we stop production energy, we will continue our imported goods, such as car parts, building materials, or all the essential tools for living. The woman and children will be the consequences because all these things are from Biafra land. The women will suffer significantly because polygamy is allowed in the north. Those who have access to money will marry an adolescent girl. We cannot allow this in the twenty-first century. This is just me thinking about what we can do to bring peace and equality to all Nigerians; all the activists complain about the government not doing enough because of the lack of equality. If the national cake is shared equally, everyone will be happy. There will be no need for the separation of Biafra from Nigeria.

Nigeria, Brazil, and India were in the same category forty years ago; these countries have gone further than Nigeria in every aspect of life. So, what happens? Sometimes I thought Nigerian leaders deliberately destroyed Nigeria so that no one would come into Nigeria and question the way they run the country. At the same time, I believe ethnicity plays a vital role in Nigeria's problem. However, I do not believe in the separation of Biafra from Nigeria. Together we can achieve the impossible.

If I am allowed to be elected as Nigeria president? This is the first thing I will do after selecting my teams. I will fight against ethnicity and abolish it. We can have Nigerian people thinking only about themselves but everyone else. There comes the hard part, how do we abolish ethnicity?

I need to build an institutional base. What is the purpose of this base? To serve the Nigerian people, the building will remind us how far we came in everything every Nigerian is going through today. One day we look back and thank those who risk everything to bring enlightenment and a better future to the people of Nigeria. That's the point of the base; in this building, everything we run Nigeria successfully is in this base, especially security and division analysis is included in the building. We must start from somewhere. Cleaning up, enhancing, and financing agriculture will be next. In doing that, we ensure enough food, clean water, and a stable environment for children to play, grow up, and go to school. I will create a new institute of law that will describe every citizen's rights in plain words and handouts. That way, everyone understands what the law says; I will also create an offline network for all Nigerians where Nigerian people can communicate or discuss problems that face their government privately. Unknowing will have no excuse for ignorance. Everyone faces or will be persecuted according to the law and entirely bear the consequences of their actions. They were supposed to know better with all information I had provided.

The next thing is to upgrade or create a payments system for all Nigerian government workers, all civil servants at any level; the system will calculate the average spending for every worker a month and multiplies it by two will be their salaries in a month, and automatic yearly increase on wages, after a particular period they you have worked for the government. What they are worth. The new institute of law will increase their wages. The same rule will apply to teachers, police, and anyone who works in the public and private sectors. You will be paid what you deserve. For example, if your rent is a minimum of #15,000 a month, you will get #120,000 monthly if you are on salary. If you are paid weekly, you will get #30,000. And if you are paid every two weeks, you will get #60,000

This new institute of law is where we will spend a lot of money because that is the core of the problem. This law is specifically designed to eradicate poverty and stop people from corrupting the system; nothing destroys a nation like back door deals and bribes; this system will force everyone to live by the rules starting with cashless payment methods. Another benefit for the people from this law will be security. We must make sure that Nigeria or Biafra is a home for everyone and that it accepts diversity. This place is where we go when the world is falling apart. This means if you are a resident of Nigeria or Biafra, you can give your residency card to someone else to live there, with conditions and according to the law. It is a place for the poor and the rich. If you are a resident of Sun City, you will be granted the opportunity to travel worldwide to research and study. Then you will return for a week every three months to share your knowledge and studies. After that, you can go to another city to obtain more information. We need a reliable source to build and make Nigeria or Biafra great through learning and understanding our civilization. Sun City is not just a city. It's the home of the gods. When I say the home of the gods, I mean home for great men and women. And for every great man and woman, more is required of them. You don't have to be rich to be great; you can be poor and still be great. So, when I call it the home of the gods, I mean the home for everyone.

We have financed agriculture and created a new law institute for civil servants. Next is financing energy sources and science, including building science centers for discovery and research. We need to find a way to make a sustainable energy source. We can use solar, which will accumulate too much land and require maintenance. There will be workers, so we don't want that; we need to find another way. We need nuclear energy. I know we have at least thermal nuclear power plants here in Canada. This is precisely what Nigeria need intends to solve energy problems in the country. There are seventy-five in the United States alone, meaning they have more energy than anyone else. If correct. Once we have steady power, we can achieve anything else.

Infrastructure projects come next. We will build roads, bridges, and cities. We will have six- and eight-year projects and all will be paid for before my team, and I leave office. We will build electric trains if we have the power source. We will first concentrate on the bigger cities, but the villages will remain behind until we can connect the village to town. The whole thing will become a paradise. My dream is to make Nigeria a paradise for everyone.

After that, we need to control the transportation system, which will add more revenue, create jobs, and bring a new local government law that will enable us to reach out to those urban areas. This will help villagers and those in the cities to understand that the rules apply to everyone, the rich and the poor. Before we clear up the roads and build bus stations and terminals for all types of transportation, we need to build factories. This includes what is necessary to transport goods and services. If we can produce more materials, we can export them abroad, the same way we export our cashews crude oil; we need to make something else to export. We need to build materials and invent something no one ever has, and the world will turn to us. So, when we establish the relationship between the world trade organizations and us. And they will listen to us, at least be able to sell our goods in the international market.

Then we will start to trade and build factories in industrial centers, including our oil, a Nigerian crude oil station formerly used for slavery in the eighteenth century. We will demolish and rebuild with newer technologies to overhaul the station and its workers and set up a new phase with an AI interface and everything required for crude oil transactions in Nigeria. All the locations will be connected, making it easier to track how much revenue comes into the country and how it affects its GDP. Then we can make our budgets, including rebuilding and financing the previously described sectors.

We will keep this going for at least three years. By then, and after the second election, we will have steady electricity to run our country efficiently. And also, we will have nuclear reactor stations up and running. The next thing is upgrading Nigeria's refineries and having direct pipelines to all NPP stations. That will keep it going; by refining our oil here at home, we will have surplus fuel to run the reactors and bring the price of gas to kobos.

We will constantly deliver and expand our technology. The goal is to find self-sustainable energy sources. Before leaving office, I will ensure our energy source is on the market. It will be an economic cash cow as everyone will want it. It can prove that anything is possible. You just have to find the core point. Any machine can run by itself without stopping. This is the target and the priority of the new Nigeria or Biafra, whichever comes first.

Suppose you ask my opinion between Nigeria and Biafra. In that case, I will tell you if the north and west can accept that Biafrans are critical to the growth of Nigeria and we can work together for Nigeria to succeed, nothing will stop us from becoming a wealthy, civilized nation.

Regarding educational and environmental development, we will pay attention to our schools, including creating new institutions, ranging from colleges to universities, apprenticeship courses, and training in every department. This will give us enough knowledgeable people to keep Nigeria running for the next eight years before handing it over to another person who will continue serving the Nigerian people.

The first thing we must do to develop Nigeria is to take a careful look at our financial situation. We need to come up with a number to develop the country without borrowing more money from the International Monetary Fund (IMF). I don't want to find Nigeria in the Ethiopian situation when we look at the overall financial situation and discover the cure is worse than the disease. When we come up with the number, we will be sure to tackle one problem at a time, not two or three. That way, we can have enough money to run the country without failing the economy and the people of Nigeria. They will know we are here to help them. If we do not do it, no one will. We are the miracle, and it's coming. We have to fix this country, all of us! I want us to work together as a gigantic team and build ourselves a better Nigeria. It's coming! Nigeria or Biafra, whichever comes first.

Next, we will concentrate on what the people need the most to access what is happening in Nigeria. We need to create a network of websites and apps also available offline. In that network, we will talk about Nigeria's problems. Everyone can be heard there. We will vote on what to do first between electricity and building roads. Those are the things we all agree on. I will make the decisions because I know exactly what needs to be done first. We will first build the infrastructure and all government roads. We need to link every village, town, and state. We need more highways and to redesign the city. Whether we are building the roads or electricity, the most important thing is that it creates jobs everywhere.

I will ask my fellow Nigerians to slow down on increasing the population. This will not be a dictatorship; it is not like the Chinese. I'm just trying to figure out how many mouths to feed. Men and women, we will work hard, be disciplined, and say no. You don't have to give someone a reason to say no to bribes and corruption. And we will try to commit more time and money to the police. We will talk with them, train them, and pay them more. They are one of the most important parts if we want the new Nigeria to succeed. They are the security. They will be happy with us and will be with us on our journey to future Nigeria or Biafra.

During the development phase, when we are building the roads, we will need a railway line that will go from Enugu City to Lagos and from Lagos to Abuja and return to the river state. As time goes on, we will link other states. Between the roads are tramways, which will connect more trains on the way as development continues. We need to give our people permanent and reliable access to transportation. A system that will not fail them and will help them restructure their lives in the new Nigeria. But we need electricity to surpass success. This railway line, in time, will be connected to cross river states in southern and eastern Nigeria.

With that, we can work at least for two years with good movement. The economy has been built up, and people will have access to money, food, and transportation. A new tax system will be introduced that will help the government revenue increments. This is Nigerian people's money, and they should know how much they contribute, where it goes, what happens to it, and so on. Everyone contributes to the purse while the government saves all its money from natural resources, including oil, coal, zinc, gold, and diamonds. We will stay under the radar while we build Nigeria for the future.

I plan to get Nigeria sustainable energy within two to three years. At least that is my plan. We will invest in solar and nuclear power, trying to save the environment as well, because when we use nuclear power, it destroys the environment. Everyone has a job in every department, private sector, and government sector, and we expect them to deliver. There will be no arguments. If there is a mistake, residents will be notified immediately. We cannot go back and fix things after tremendous damage. Once we have sustainable energy and the electricity is distributed correctly, this is where we will begin. We will stay two hundred miles from any nuclear site. We will build our factories for production, where we will test our abilities and knowledge. Building our factories will allow the young and bright children access training, learning, and practicing. We want to give them the best as the future of new Nigeria; when families do well, the kids turn out great, and we will empower our women to participate anywhere they see fit. And we can all build Nigeria or Biafra together.

Let's face our challenges; this is the bad news. The bad news is that the international community might not stop interfering in our national affairs. So, we have to deal with this problem because we are suffering, and they are not. We will start producing our things and stop importing what we can make. This is the most crucial part of reestablishing and growing Nigeria's economy. Unlike before, Nigeria imported 90 percent of its products from abroad. This time we will have our products, the things we need. As I said, we will import what we need, like medical equipment, that we might not be able to produce, at least not yet, at this time. So, this is important.

What if the international community continues its interference and threats? We must tackle that problem because this is a psychological and financial war. The other way around is to fight it and win. There is no other way. When I said fight, I mean we need a fair agreement between Nigeria and the international community, not like the one the English did to benefit them when they created Nigeria. Even if you sneak away, they keep looking for something to bring us down. Fight Western global politics and gain financial independence; free from the debt, we do not know how it was borrowed or what it's to be used for, a debt in which the interest rate higher than the amount borrowed. We do not want interference from the outside world anymore. If they disagree with our price, they can buy elsewhere.

However, some things will remain the same, and oil prices will. I am trying to say that Westerners buy our oil at a low cost, and due to corruption, the NNPC—who is not supposed to be in charge of selling the oil but only producing it—is charged with selling and making at the same time. So, most of the money got lost, and we couldn't pay our debts or care for our country. The government official has foreign accounts with millions of stolen cash. This issue will be addressed as well. And if the international community does not abide by our policies, we will let the world know what is happening. There is no other choice.

Another thing we need to take into account is unexpected situations and problems from communities, tribes, and lands. While working together, we will encounter these problems and need to learn as we go. It's a one-way shot for Nigeria. If we wait for more time, we will fail and need to wait for another twenty years to try again. We all must stick together. If Biafra gets its republic, then I will work with Biafra on this idea. So, we address the problems as they come.

We must reform the Supreme Court by adjusting our national and security defense systems. This system will help us address our prison system and development. And if our children make mistakes, we will give them second chances. All our prisons will be built on farms. Instead of locking our children in cells because they have committed crimes, we will have a particular prison more like rehab where they will work on a farm or learn something new, training them to rethink and giving them second chances. They will be going to work every day and getting paid. It won't be the same as minimum wage, but it will help them save some money. They can help their children outside with school supplies, for example. With this standard-setting, their minds will be rethinking. It will be like a camp, but they are free. They will also have access to the outside world through TVs. When they get out, they will know if they are against it or for it. This system will help straighten Nigeria's justice system and guarantee a fair trial for everyone.

Communication standards are another problem we must tackle. We need to find a way to understand communications more from the ground up. Foreign companies are running communications systems in Nigeria. Billions of dollars are supposed to go to the Nigerian government, but the money goes abroad, draining the country's finances even more. We are creating a new Nigerian communication law to help control the whole communication system and relieve us of private companies. Any foreign companies who want to continue doing business with our country will stand as an affiliation or agreement on both sides. If they refuse, we pay them off and let them pack and go.

But before we do this, we need to understand how the communication system works so we can build ours from the ground up. This is another challenge that will come. CEOs and executives with access to companies and governments that can shut us down can also benefit from this. As I said, my people, this is a war we cannot afford to lose. Our children cannot suffer anymore. Enough is enough. We are moving on. Come to Nigeria and fight us if you are looking for a war. It is a war you don't want to start. We just want to fix our problems. We do not need your help. If you have something we want, we will buy it from you. If you refuse to sell it to us, we will improvise. I will make Igbo boys from my tribe build the machine you refuse to sell to us because my boys can do anything in this world. To tell you the truth, we are not afraid of you. We are all in this, all Nigerians. We Nigerians will work day and night to make Nigeria a better country.

Another problem we must tackle is agricultural upgrading. We need to upgrade all machines and help farmers with upgraded fertilization techniques. One of the significant problems in the Nigerian agricultural system is the need to control livestock on farms. This means we must map out a chunk of land with good vegetation and a water system and place our farmers there. Not everyone will be able to farm; you will need a certificate. Don't worry about workers. This is where the prison will be built, and the prisoners will help farm and harvest food. They do their time; they come out, and so on.

Every farmer will be responsible for their livestock, including moving them from location to location. Farmers must fence their livestock, so they don't damage other people's farms. These are the problems we need to tackle and one of the many problems Nigerians have.

Another thing we will do—the essential part of building one Nigeria or Biafra—Niger Delta must be recognized and well paid for their oil. Their opinion will be on the table, and its request for development and the mines will be negotiated, no longer ignored. We will make sure that Niger Delta benefits from its resources as the origin. I am glad General Sani Abacha, the former head of state, built the pipeline that traveled from south to north. Every Nigerian will have access to Nigeria's resources.

My target is 2030 when I take over as Nigerian president. These things will be done. It's a promise. That is eight years from now. I have enough time to gather energy and resources.

We also need to refine our belief system. I am not saying I don't believe in God; I do. I am just saying that there are thousands of churches, and do we need that many? No. All the pastors will be allowed to enroll in research of knowledge, like philosophy or psychology. Those who know how to heal can put their research in words and descriptions. That way, there will be churches, but there will only be one or two to share, not thousands of churches all over the place. I am not saying I am against God. We need to wise up and place people in good areas where they can make a difference in their unique abilities.

The Catholic church collects money from poor people and sends it to the Vatican to develop and enrich its agendas. That also disgusts me; it is not what the Bible says we should do. That is why we will ask all the Catholic churches to participate in the fundraising campaigns to create a new Nigeria. This fundraising will be conducted by the Nigerian government and private sectors in charge of charitable organizations. We will then know the money is coming to us directly and into Nigerian people's purses and pockets. We will invite members of all the Catholic churches and oil company executives, including Dangote, one of the wealthiest men in Nigeria. Together we will raise money. We are not asking the Catholic church to leave Nigeria; we want them to stay based on the new agreement; any money taken from the Nigerian people should be spent on developing schools and amenities. They build Catholic schools in many countries in the Western world with the money it collects from the poor in Africa, especially the poor people of Nigeria. That will be their contribution to the new Nigeria. If they refuse to acknowledge the request or raise funds with us during the fundraising meeting, the Catholic church will not be part of the new Nigeria. There I said it.

So, if you are a Catholic, we will build our brand of Catholicism and not send money to the Vatican. It's the same God and system. We already have black priests. The same procedure applies to the Muslims in the north.

Everything will be restructured to favor the Nigerian people. We will suffer no more; we are done suffering. If suffering is dues, this nation has paid. If action is required to free ourselves from the propaganda this world has dumped on us over the years, then that is what we will do. Political and economic crises have thrown us to the bottom of the barrel, and the world blames us for not being responsible for our people. We will not allow it anymore, and we had enough. It is time. Nigerians, it's time. We are paying for crimes we did not commit. What do you think will happen with climate change if the world does not change? I'll tell you what will happen.

It will destroy the entire planet. Who caused the problem of climate change? The Western world they are benefiting from it. We are suffering as well, and they are profiting from our suffering. So, the sooner we build our nation to stand tall, the sooner we will enjoy it with them. Why should we not want to enjoy the planet? So that's what happens when we fail.

The international community known as G8 and G7 will continue to enjoy what they created at the expense of everyone else. Look at Sri Lanka, for example. Almost 70 percent of its land is a swamp. Do you think Sri Lanka is the cause of this problem? Of course not; They have nothing to do with it. Nor did they have a clue of where the problem came from, not until later on when scientists started to discover evidence about what caused the problem. The ice is melting, and when the ice melts, that is more water. And the water has to go somewhere. Sri Lanka is a victim of a high temperature created by humankind through industrialization and nuclear radiation that increase the planet's temperature, melting the ice.

In today's world, a man's character is everything; my advice, especially to young people, is to keep your dreams alive and not let anyone take them away. If you have to fight for it and die, it is honorable death because, in the end, you die fighting for what you believe in. I believe it's better to fight for my dreams and die and still die without fighting for it; everyone dies in the end?" Death is inevitable. My point is that if the planet is burned out by solar flames, high temperatures, or excess water because of human error. Some people are using the opportunity to enjoy life and take advantage of the suffering of people in other parts of the world—who are paying the ultimate price for a crime they did not commit—should they not fight it? We all know the truth. Sri Lanka will not fight the Western world for suffering for their mistakes or the rest devasted countries; the least the developed world should do is compensate them.

I am against violence, but war ranges in every part of the globe; if you have natural resources, your life is in danger; why? At what end does it stop? Do you know? Living beautifully would be the easiest thing to do on Earth. If we can find a way to love one another and to be fair from one human to another, when I say fight for what is right? I do not mean with violence, but through negotiations and consensus, I know the developed world needs oil more than we do, and we need industrialization equipment more than they do. So, let's start there; let's trade. Don't be okpakuerieri, who took everything from the poor, sit on your beach house, and has it all, but for? He had acres of land and strippers, living a joyful life at the expense of the suffering of others. We Nigerians cannot be part of it. We want to fix our problems and sell our products mainly to Africans. We need to be allowed to do our bidding. Suppose foreign countries want to buy our products, excellent. I look forward to that. We can buy from them, and all is well, but they can't buy from us? How is that fair? I will give you a typical example of how we have been treated. A young graduate will come from Nigeria to some western countries that speak English with a degree and will be told your education level is not accepted. You have to start all over again. Thanks to Dr. Olumuyiwa igbalajobi, who requested Alberta university to remove Nigeria from the list of countries that are supposed to write language tests before seeking admission. Thanks, Canada, for listening. Only if the world is like Canada will this planet be the paradise God intended. Now you understand my pain; let's get real for a second; the developed world and world market could choose to stop interfering in Nigerian affairs so we can repair the damage that has been done over the years; since there is like a sinking ship, just let us be, leave us alone. Now China is all over Africa in the name of investing that doesn't befit African people; another future problem to deal with.

Let's be clear everyone knows what's going on in Africa but chooses to keep quiet; let's leave it at that; the time for Africa will come; for now, let's focus on Nigeria. We are not showing the world what they are doing to us or expecting them to help us; they have contributed to our problems. To be honest, we're not blaming anyone for our problems. We just ask to be left alone. This is the first time I have raised my voice. We will no longer be humiliated by W.T.O. So, when they try to berate us, we will not stop. We will continue to fight for what is ours. We want to fix our problems. Just leave us alone. Other countries have been interfering in our governing system and haven't been able to improve our situation for the last sixty years. We have to set our own. That is all I am saying.

However, we must also strengthen Nigeria's healthcare system. We will begin with government hospitals, starting with renovations and infrastructure upgrades. While doing that, we will consult all the private hospitals in Nigeria for fair contract bids for each geographic location, which will be taken over as government contractors. The hospitals will be used to treat everyone who comes in. The government will pay them by the hour and supply equipment. We will all work together. Private hospitals will play vital roles, just like the police service. We will listen to the demands and proposals from every private sector that has something to contribute to improving Nigeria. Requests will be made to Nigerians who reside abroad with experience in various positions. We will negotiate salaries based on experience and motivations. We need to know if we are building a new Nigeria everyone will enjoy and, therefore, Nigeria's civilization to carry on to the next generation, or if we want to remain as we are. And that is where the motivation comes in. When I finish my job building a new Nigeria, my challenge will be who takes over from me and continue the excellent work I have started. Before leaving office. That's another challenge; I must choose the best candidate to take the lead. Otherwise, all my hard with will go down the drain.

While I am still the president of Nigeria, I will design a program that will allow particular healthier and smarter politicians who can run for president and have good intentions for Nigeria. I am talking about endorsing someone who is not necessarily only politically inclined but also an excellent judge of character; it excludes dubious politicians and their offspring who emerge from colonialism. Instead, a person who will continue the excellent work I left behind. We need three consecutive presidents with the same ideas as mine. That will give us twenty-four years, and Nigeria will be set free and recognized like every other country in the world. So, this program will be agreed on by my administration, the Senate, the House of Representatives, and all the traditional rulers of every tribe. This program gives us twenty-four years of prosperity and government management, and with this, we can build a new Nigeria or Biafra. If we can, we will make it through twenty-four years, and Nigeria will be set free. We have no choice; the Chinese are coming; they are already here in Africa; Nigeria needs to be prepared so it is not too late like when the Europeans arrived.

Another thing my administration will do is introduce government-free housing (GFH). This will include shelters for women, the disabled, and seniors. It's a similar system as in Canada but uses a different method. I was planning on using my money to build shelters in Enugu City. I gave them a private school for GS1 to SS3. I did the best I could based on the resources I had. It takes a long time and lots of hard work to help a community. I started to think about how to get the pool of Nigerian wealth so I could distribute it accordingly and help people who deserve it and need it the most. That is why becoming the president of Nigeria came to mind. I am not here for the money. I am here to make the world know we exist too. If I were here for money, I wouldn't come. I am a businessman and have enough money for myself and my family. Instead, I want to help my people and their families so they can enjoy the same things other families abroad enjoy, mostly from their suffering. I say we suffer no more. That is it! We are done! And this is my vow to the Nigerian people when I become president.

We need to acknowledge that there will be unknown challenges. Unknown challenges are like maggots: They can destroy you from the inside out. Every incident and every suspicious activity must be reported. This is not to say that a person in charge is incompetent. It is the other way around. Reporting mistakes and errors will help us better learn and understand how our system is working. So, we will report every near miss and accident in the system.

This is the only information I have on how to make Nigeria or Biafra a better country for now, and I believe they deserve it. It is the country's right to enjoy its resources.

Now that we have completed all the ideas and protocols, it's time for the second phase. In this phase, we further create a division of labor for ministers and break down accountabilities. Doing so will help us identify errors and grasp what went wrong.

Let's begin with the law enforcement agency. The institute needs guidance, so we are creating a separate division. This division will consist of civilians with the capacity to fire any law enforcement personnel who refuse to follow the rules of law. This can range from the police chief to sergeants' significant generals. Each state in Nigeria will provide and organize its executive division, which oversees law enforcement agencies. Their job is to ensure that law enforcement personnel do their jobs correctly. In this division, anyone who has been neglected or mistreated according to the law can complain to this administrative division.

Civilians can be appointed, elected, or handpicked by the state governor based on their reputations and references.

Agriculture.

The most important part is the agricultural system. We need to maximize the status of the agriculture minister because from agriculture comes the confusion and disagreements that cause conflicts in environmental development. We need to create a division allowing the agriculture minister to hire more workers and representatives in different locations. Local governments will appoint representatives to check for environmental violations in person. These representatives will report to the local governments, who will report to the chief executives. The executive will finalize the report to the minister. The Minister of Agriculture's office will be responsible for correcting the mistakes or taking the matter to the next step if needed. The same rule applies to all the ministries, such as finance, natural resources, energy and mining, and Healthcare.

But what happens if Nigeria does not agree with my ideas or proposals? Then they leave me with no choice but to break off Biafra and make her a republic. To do this, we must play smart and avoid war and violence. The question is, how can we convince Nigeria to grant Biafra her independence without bloodshed or war? We have tried to do that for sixty years, begging and pleading with the international community for support and help. But there was no response. So, asking for help from global communities is pointless. How about sitting down with the Biafran and the Nigerian governments and finding common ground from which we can work together and benefit from it equally? Candidates from different tribes, such as Igbo or Southern Nigeria, contesting for the presidency and fair elections conducted without prejudice, everyone working together for a better Nigeria or Biafra is an option.

Another option is to avoid asking the international community— for example, Israel, China, Russia, Europeans, or the United States for help. We know the United States won't help us but instead cause more catastrophe. So, we will deal with the Nigerian government based on natural resources. We can sell to them at half the market price for a period based on our agreed-upon consensus. There will be free transit through the borders for vehicles carrying essential goods for human consumption. This deal will be implemented when we become a free country. That way, Nigeria can play the part of can play the role the United States plays with Canada. We have to find common ground without bloodshed so everyone benefits.

Biafra is ignorant of the rule of law, while Nigeria suffers lousy governance. Biafra is very good at governing, so Nigeria doesn't allow Biafrans to be selected as presidential candidates to rule Nigeria. Fear of separation, and that increase the suffering of Nigeria's people. This is another option.

And if either of those doesn't work, the third option is war. And war, as we all know, is a shameful thing. It's not just the military that suffers. Everyone will suffer, including the innocent, women, and children. They will die for this cause, so we must find common ground to fix the problem. Biafrans have been abandoned for years and left with nothing. Not after the civil war left 2 million Biafrans dead; 80 percents were women and children who died from starvation. We cannot allow that to happen again. Not to Biafra. And not even to Nigeria, who caused the problem, or any other country. We cannot go to war; we need to unite. Those who want independence can have it.

I have learned something so far during my travel as an African scholar and potential anthropologist. The only way to achieve peace in any country or continent is to speak the same language and dialect. If you want peace, let Biafra be on its own, and let the Yorubas have their republic, the Hausas. These tribes have different languages and are packed together as one. Because of the language barrier, we often misunderstand each other. This is my suggestion to all African nations. Those who seek independence shall have it; that way, we can all be at peace. If the Nigerian government can see the truth in what I am saying, we can all achieve peace and solve this problem without bloodshed.

Biafra and Nigeria must consider the consequences of starting a new government in this global political economy in the twenty-first century. So we have to understand the consequences. It's not just about Biafra getting her independence. Let's talk about Nigeria when Biafra is gone.

Nigeria will be no more, or another tribe will take Nigeria's name as their own. But what happens to the people? I understand the problem will be more significant than fighting a war. You will have one hundred million people displaced all over the country without direction, governance, or laws. By then, everyone will try to be independent. As soon as Biafra gains her independence, the rest of the tribes will want to have their independence. What happens, then? There will be no rule of law. I am Biafran, and based on what my people and I have been through at the hands of the Nigerian government, I shouldn't feel sorry for them. It shouldn't be my concern to worry about people who starved almost a million children to death while the world kept quiet. Nobody said anything or tried to help us. They only try to help when it benefits them. But this is the new world. This is the future. We will not allow people to starve to death.

Let's assume the Nigerian and the Biafran governments conclude that Biafra should be granted her independence. We need to set two plans in motion to protect Nigerians when we are gone and to help build the Biafran nation without interference from anyone. The problem is not that Nigeria didn't want Biafra to get her independence. The problem is what will happen to her after we are gone. Most of the resources in Nigeria come from Biafra. For example, zinc, cement, oil, and coal come from Biafra land. This was their fear. When these plans are in motion, how about we offer them something? As I said, we can give them international goods for half price, but that is not enough.

After Biafra gains her independence, the Hausas will become Nigeria. They are farmers and don't possess as much education as the easterners and the westerners. But if the westerners choose to remain in Nigeria with the Hausas, that will make the job easier for me. I don't need to implement the two laws in motion. They can work together, and Biafra will have time to build her nation. When we gain our independence, Biafra and Oduduwa will have a policy that allows them to have the same benefits as Nigeria; Oduduwa will also need help to build their nation. It will be their first independence. Throughout the years, the Yorubans have not been interested in having freedom. They just want to be Nigerian and spend the nation's money unnecessarily, and most of Nigeria's money is in personal offshore accounts. That caused this problem in the first place.

How can we make Biafra great? To make Biafra great, we need to be recognized by the world. We need to invent something to help humanity, something everyone wants. It is the only way the world will see us. I am writing this book in the era of Donald Trump as president of the United States, the Chinese dictator, and during COVID-19. I always believed that former US President Barack Obama would help the whole world unite, but he failed. If Obama had finished his job, I would not have been writing this book. But he ignored Africa during his time as president, doing nothing for us. To make matters worse, during his presidency, Libya's collapse ended the life of Muammar Gaddafi of Libya, the candlelight in the darkness, and the hope for a better Africa. And here comes Donald Trump, a businessman, not a politician, leading the world in the wrong direction. We must understand what I am saying. Hypothetically, let's assume Donald Trump did not turn the world around and make America just for Americans. The world would be in chaos, and Nigeria is not doing anything to prepare itself for what was coming. Imagine if the oil runs out. I know oil will be needed, but not as much as it is needed right now. What will countries like Nigeria do? Countries that depend on oil to survive will be in chaos. If I were in Nigeria, I would start prepping myself. This is why we need to take action before it is too late. We need to invest our money wisely, preferably in something to sustain ourselves without oil.

For Biafra to be recognized by the whole world, they needed to invent something that no one had ever seen. The first thing is to build a science center that will only be for those capable of creating. A scholarship will be given to those who qualify; this will be one of the benefits of the Minister of education divisions. The education division will be responsible for choosing students who are intelligent and capable of the invention to participate in the science center. This is how we will find people who can create and invent something the world has never seen.

Another thing I will do for Biafra is to upgrade their mentality. People must understand that we are living in a new world. We must show that things cannot always be the same. You cannot beat someone to death because they stole a loaf of bread. Citizens must alert law enforcement to deal with the matter according to the rule of law, not taking matters into their own hands. In addition, I have to show the value of human life. Life is precious and essential, and you can't kill someone just like that. Human life is more valuable than anything else in the world. These are mentalities that need to be understood and practiced.

The same thing applies to every living thing on earth. It doesn't matter where you come from. Everyone will be treated equally and respected. Equality will be our modern invention. It is the only thing that will count to Biafra. Equality will be the icon of Biafra. "The land of the free," Biafra will be known as "the land of equality." It will be where everyone is recognized and respected, despite their faith.

The most important thing I will do if elected president of Biafra or Nigeria is to channel resources and access to the Biafran or Nigerian government to focus on the poor, the orphans, the widows, and the disabled. They are the ones no one pays attention to. That will be reversed and taken care of equally. Biafra must understand respect for human life, acknowledgment of supremacy, and the consequences of wrongdoing. With all this, Biafra can be a country.

My administration will focus on creating a stable relationship with all African countries. We must find common ground where we can work together and develop Africa. We owe that to Mother Africa. Since Nigeria will be the center of excellence, we will push the transportation of goods and production. Sales of essential needs are a priority. They will feature products produced by Africans and used by Africans. No offense here; we are just trying to survive. There will be missionaries for farming and industrial businesses. We will build a great nation by teaching and training these countries on how to survive. It will be called the African Region. The government agencies will be in charge of everything, including where all natural resources are sold. There are fifty-two countries in the continent, and we will negotiate on behalf of every African nation on what will be sold to us, what is to be accepted, who is coming into the African Region, and who is leaving. This will give us a look at every quadrant, allowing us to monitor what is happening on our continent. The relationship between African nations will be transparent. We must share information equally if we are going to survive. The world is moving on, and we must be part of it. We must be ready. If Africa is remembered in the new world, we should be ready now. It is better to be prepared than not to be prepared. If worse comes to worst, at least we know Africa will survive.

Chapter 13

Ogbanje

I have reached true greatness in this murky world of uncertainty. Two worlds exist in different spaces and times, in the multiverses unknown to human eyes. There is not even an acknowledgment of their existence. I have reached greatness in this place where time does not change or exist, and information flows through a timeline from different dimensions. In my world of ogbanje, traveling through time is the same as flying in a dream world, where messages are passed through to me concerning Planet Earth, about the things to come, like the new system implant-control warning. I don't know how to explain it more, but something is coming. Time is upon us. Embrace the impact.

Does a time machine exist? Not that I know of, at least not now. What if I told you that a time machine is not impossible to build if you know where to start? In the dream world, a time machine has something to do with rivers and canoes on earth. While in the multiverse, there is a star, a transforming star, which has different symbols. It changes as it pumps out something completely different. From all the stars I have seen, some are shaped like forks or spoons. Some are shaped like turtles, and others like triangles and oranges.

There are all different shapes. I haven't seen a symbol like that since heaven split into two parts.

The question is if I know the future since I can travel through time to different worlds—like a flying dream world, where one night in the real world equals six months in the dream world—what else can I do? I have never seen a time machine in the dream world because I am the time machine. Every human being is capable of transcending and can look beyond our consciousness to gaze at what is on the other side, between the stars. Some nights when the Creator finds me worthy, he will touch my shoulder and show me the beauty of all creation. The same goes for you. He'll ask, "What do you think, you who say I don't exist? You who say God is dead. You ask why I didn't answer when you called upon me."

When we dream, our souls leave our bodies and travel somewhere far away or closer. The soul travels in real time. In some cases, people don't remember their dreams. But journeying across the heavens and the universe has revealed the truth about creation. How long would they tell you something otherwise? When you tell them the truth, they ask if it has been scientifically proven. That's just an excuse to hold someone accountable and ignore reality. My father always tells us the stories of our ancestors who lived on mountaintops thousands of years ago and how they traveled through lightning and thunderstorms, known today as wormholes. At the very top of the mountain is a circle made with stones and red mud. Who knows its purpose? It has been there from the beginning of time.

One day I decided to see the circle myself. So, I went to the mountaintop to see if the ring was still there and if my father was telling the truth. To my surprise, it was still there. I imagined many of them could have been built in that specific location. The second time I visited that mountain, I realized the circle was made precisely in the center. Standing there, I could see the whole village. I said, "This circle has to be some kind of platform for a ship or something else out of the ordinary."

According to my father, there are four rules to command thunderstorms and lightning in the story. The words are in an ancient language only the father speaks. He has a mark like a tattoo on his forehead, just four lines. My father told me my grandfather has the same pattern on his forehead, passed on from his father and others before him. The rules predict where the lightning and thunder begin when it comes back and what it takes on their way out. Why? Because if you command lightning to go somewhere, to harm someone, or to destroy a house, you must keep something equivalent to what you ask it to do when it bounces back, like positive and negative energies. In this case, this is more complex than traditional ancient methods. When lightning bounces back, and there is nothing for it to take, it will take your life. Everyone knows that lightning comes before a thunderstorm. Maybe that's how it works.

If I knew what I know now, I would convince my father to teach it to me. And I would guard it with my life. When I asked my father who built the circle, he said it was the enslaved people from across the sea many years ago. So many times, I begged him to teach me the ancient language. He refused each time. He always said, "The next generations are wicked. They will use power for evil." And so it was. When he died, the knowledge died with him and is now gone forever.

There are some things in this world that we have clear pictures of. And there are things we have no idea what they are. Every day we search for clues to lead us to the ultimate answer to who we are. And yet no one has an accurate explanation of where we come from. Every theory is based on hypotheses. Over time people begin to believe it is the truth, even though they know in the back of their heads that it is all based on someone's idea of what they think might be the truth. Tell a person something more than twenty-eight times, and it will begin to sound like the truth. After a while, I realized there was no answer to the question that had been asked. There is just us and the universe for now. It's just a question and an answer, so let's leave it alone and continue our lives. Besides, life is too short. We should not spend our entire lives seeking the truth in humankind's eyes. If we were meant to know our origins scientifically, we would have learned by now with all our technologies. And yet no one has an accurate answer to who we are.

The answer doesn't matter anymore. We are children of God, believe it or not. We are not bastards, even though the result might help us understand everything around us. But what would life be like if we saw God personally? I don't know. How would the world react if someone saw God, not just his existence? What would it be like? Since we can see God now, we don't have to go to work or do anything else, right? He is the One who created us; we're his responsibility. Or maybe we rebel against God to take control of our lives. And trust me, sometimes it sucks to hand your life over to God, whom you can't see physically. What would life be like? What do you think will happen in everything we know and believe in society? Whatever happens, it can't be good. And that puts me at a top level. But like I said, the answer doesn't matter anymore. That is unfortunate, very unfortunate. To understand the fundamental reason for life, you need to understand life first. You can't have one without the other.

If you ask me where the earth's center is, I would answer, "I don't think it is among the stars." No, human beings are the centers of the universe. Believe it or not, the universe wouldn't have existed if human beings were not here to acknowledge its existence and see the infinite universe with both eyes to understand the dream and real worlds. So it is my conclusion that the center of the universe is the human heart. Within the human mind is a connection between the universe and human beings. Because of that relationship, human beings are capable of transcending to high purposes of life. But I am afraid we may wreck Mother Earth before reaching our true potential. Like my mother always says, "Don't break the plate before the food is ready," I fear that's what will happen to human beings if they do not change their ways. I believe human beings will reach the greatest civilization and conquer the stars. But if we continue in the direction we are going, our food will be ready and will be no plates to serve it on. When we become the greatest civilization that ever existed and physically conquered the universe, we may have no place to call home. That's my fear for humankind.

There is nothing wrong with success or earning the most significant achievement in human history, as long as success doesn't surpass knowledge, even though expertise and hit have the same pattern, like an implant, to pass on to the next generation. Imagine if I had the power to fly in the real world. That would be excellent knowledge to pass on to my children. What is knowledge without success? Knowledge without success is like a eunuch with a beautiful bride. Knowledge can be imprisoned for a very long time without success. But without success, knowledge has no power.

To free your knowledge requires free will and success, not just in the dream world but also in the real world. Sometimes I wish I had power in the real world as I do in the dream world to free my knowledge and pass it on to the world, not just my children. Going to a park is free will, and it is normal. You desire to travel somewhere else, meet people with different faces, names, and lifestyles, learn from each other and pass on what was known to a future generation. That is free will.

But a flying dream is a gift I wish everyone could experience and enjoy in their lives here on earth, a place for all of us to escape from this reality, especially for those who cannot get a good night's sleep. Flying dreams will tempt you not to wake up. But when you wake up, try comparing the dream world to real life. Follow the patterns and narrations of the dream, and see if you understand what is happening around you. Imagine if we fly across all the galaxies in the universe without moving. Just in your bed, in one night, you pass through many galaxies; you love to experience flying dreams. Wouldn't that be an extraordinary achievement? This is my wish for humankind.

As an ogbanje child, life is not always easy. Every day brings different challenges from your parents and everyone else in the village. As a child, I always thought the fundamental aspect of life was to perform miracles on others, give a helping hand, sit with the poor and give them hope. Hope is the most beautiful thing and spiritual nourishment for someone's soul. And God would send someone from far or near to connect with, sail across the stars, watch the sunrise and sunset, and enjoy the world's beauty. As I grew older, I learned that it was not the same as when I was a child. I watched my children grow from tiny human beings to full-grown men. I wish them prosperity and long lives. My children hold the most important parts of my life. Daddy loves you both. Nevertheless, I saw everyone rushing, overcompensating, and bragging, which confuses things and obstructs those who follow the center point of the axis of life and happiness, and now everybody wanted it yesterday. Morality is considered a foolish thing to do.

This brings us to the lowest note of the high, as the highest note of the common. I am trying to say that the rich and the poor are equal in the eyes of God. You cannot have one without the other. But in the real world, things are slightly different between the poor and the rich. Every wealthy person can justify their richness and have to keep it all to themselves. Especially when today's religious leaders and governments are failing the people, pandemics are killing mostly our grandmas and granddads, and drugs and alcohol rampage our cities, bringing more and more poverty. My advice is to keep reinventing yourself. Do not compare yourself with others. Instead, try to help them understand life the way you do. Hopefully, that will stimulate them mentally and help sustain their lives. Individualism is cancer. You can kill someone, and the person dies quickly. But individualism is a sickness you can't kill. That is a fact. Everyone wants someone or something to enslave. It is a disease of the heart and mind that comes from within. The only way to eradicate it is to replace it with a beautiful desire. That's the difference between the animal and us.

On the other hand, we find ways to establish consistency in our lives, so we do not doubt ourselves or face the disappointment of our doings, especially when we expect more from others who have already accepted defeat without even trying. There is a way we can save everyone and help them to recognize and understand a simple truth: It is stupid to take more than what you need. What are you going to do with all that money? So, you can save for ten generations while the whole country is suffering from starvation caused by you and your greed and selfishness. One person doesn't need to have seven billion dollars when ten million people have five million among them. This is the ideology that has destabilized the whole world for a long time now. Even the Bible tells us, "What shall it profit a man to gain the whole world and lose his soul." What's the point? You can be a billionaire during your time on earth, but you can only consume what you need. That is it. What is the benefit of gaining the whole world and losing your soul?

Why can't you see that if you take exactly what you need, there will be leftovers for others in need? If everyone can see what I know, we will not only thrive but prosper in health, loving each other and helping our planet simultaneously. And our home world will recover from the abuse of money.

Unknowns are my most considered adversary because of my drive to know, the hunger to know the things I don't know, to understand my place in the universe, and to see the answer to all the formations, especially when it comes from the dream world. The most challenging part is keeping track of my recurring dreams until I write down or use a voice-recording device, which in my case, I often lose from time to time. The flying dreams I share with you are just the ones I remember entirely wholly. There is one flying dream in particular in which the information was cut in half. I think goals are vital to the human race. I didn't write about it in this book because I can't remember the end. It's lost in my memory bank. Nights like that usually happen when friends invite me over, or I go to a party or a boys' night out for a drink, tell stories of all kinds, and talk to girls. Nights like that in flying dreams are incomplete.

There was a time when I had too much information flowing from flying dreams to the real world. It's hard to keep up. Trying to remember takes energy. There are many of them, so I set a principle that any dreams I cannot remember are not meant to be told, no matter how tempting it is to remember. It's like when you want to learn something, but your mind can't remember what it was. That's the feeling I get when my dream is cut in half and why I created the principle not to chase incomplete dreams. There is a dream about dragons and the smoke that chokes people. I can't remember the end, and that's why it is not included in this book. Besides, since I can't find out how it all went down, it's better to have a complete dream than an incomplete one.

Everything is now in my favor. The rain is usually a sign of bad days ahead, especially if I am planning to embark on a journey, to fly in the dreams without falling, you must sleep facing the sky. And make sure your arms and shoulders are straight without folding. The same rules apply in the real world; if you have a job interview, you should prepare yourself days before the interview date and check out the address. Nine out of ten, if you prep yourself prior, you most likely will get the job.

To those of you who stand for the goodness of this world, I bless you. For those who sacrifice everything for the betterment of others, I bless you. There is no joy in living a life of luxury while watching others suffer to death.

We are supposed to be the best of all humankind, not just in our homes but worldwide. I say no more wars among humans. And please, no more hate. We're children of God, created in his image to thrive in every aspect of creation. This world was given to us to manage and cultivate—no more wars. There have already been too many deaths over the years. We can do better; I know we can. Look at me, for example. With the limited resources I have, I have done beautiful things. Imagine what we can accomplish when we work together.

I have achieved greatness in tight spots and conquered enemies who will stop at nothing until they see me go. Just imagine if the whole world joined together, rich and poor. In fewer than a hundred years, we could save the planet and give our grandchildren a millennium of years to inherit and enjoy the earth. All world leaders, please take a step back and consider what you are doing to the less fortunate. See if you are a great king or a Nebuchadnezzar who thinks his authority reaches all the heavens, forgetting that the same worm that keeps the poor alive is the same worm that keeps him busy.

We still have time to change, make a difference in the world, and give hope where there is no hope with pure hearts and loving kindness. To understand flying dreams from a real-world perspective, you must acknowledge the existence of goals. In the same way, human interaction with one another is how we were created, and we need each other to exist. Plans wouldn't exist without the real world. One tree cannot make a forest, no matter how big it grows. They need each other to create forests, I know how we were brought up plays a vital role in our life, but you can change. You can choose to be a guardian to all human beings. You can choose to be anything and anyone you want to be. You alone can decide who you are. No one can tell you who you are. All answers and questions end up in one place.

But what happens after we die? No one knows. We are curious about where we come from and what happens after we die. We have searched all over the universe, space, and time, looking for answers while the answer is right under our noses the whole time. Why not be kind to each other if you can, or try to because you love God, your heart is pure, or do it because you love humankind? Do it just in case everything the book of God says is true. Think of it like an insurance policy for your soul.

And yet most of us refuse to accept the simple truth that most of the things they told us were lies. To make matters worse, the movie industry has changed many concepts from its original purpose. Please, brothers and sisters who believe in the higher purpose of life, stand together.

As my teaching in this book ends, I pray that life is good to you. Be at peace with yourself and with one another.

Sleep in peace tonight, and fly in the dream world. The Creator of the universe is more significant than anything you will ever face in life. Until we meet again, I wish you true love and happiness. Let those close to you be kind to you in manners. Let the haters love you beyond all love, and may your light shine the brightest. Have this in your heart until all humans accept each other in love and kindness. Without it, humankind will never see God or reach its full potential.

This is my story in my own words.

For the whole world, we pray for a better future.

We pray for forgiveness for all humans and their transgressions against each other.

For wars against developing nations, we pray for reconciliation.

For those who have been enslaved, we pray for the forgiveness of the past.

For the wrongfully accused, innocent prisoners, we pray for their release.

We pray for a new beginning with pure hearts and love for the heartbroken ones.

For the sick, we pray for healing and new life.

For pregnant women, we pray for good health for both mother and child.

And above all, for all the children of this world, may you live in a peaceful world without hate or desolation, your future is filled with joy and happiness, and the love of the universe be your footstool.

Printed in the United States
by Baker & Taylor Publisher Services

Printed in the United States
by Baker & Taylor Publisher Services